THE HOUR
BEFORE MIDNIGHT

THE HOUR
BEFORE MIDNIGHT

A Novel of Suspense

VELDA JOHNSTON

DODD, MEAD & COMPANY
New York

1 2 3 4 5 6 7 8 9 10

Library of Congress Cataloging in Publication Data

Johnston, Velda
The hour before midnight.

I. Title.
PZ4.J7238Hm [PS3560.0394] 813'.5'4 78-1316
ISBN 0-396-07565-7

To the memory of Verna Miles

THE HOUR
BEFORE MIDNIGHT

PROLOGUE

HALF AN HOUR earlier the light filling this stone-walled room had seemed to him the cool gray of an overcast morning. But that was before the two brawny men had bound him to the heavy oak chair and fastened a knotted cord around his head. Now, because tiny blood vessels in his eyeballs had burst, the room appeared to swim in a red haze.

"Confess it, Mark. You did lie with the Lady."

His interrogator, like both his torturers, stood behind him, but in his mind's eye he could still see the thin figure in the fur-trimmed long gown of brown wool, and the cold face beneath the flat cap of brown velvet.

"I did not lie with her." Let them kill him. He would never betray her. Never!

A flat stick had been thrust between the back of Mark's head and the encircling knotted cord. One of the burly men gave the stick another twist. The knots bit deeper into Mark's forehead, widening the splits in his skin.

"Do not be a fool, Mark. I intend to have a signed confession to give to the King. If you will not sign it then someone will sign it for you. It is all one to us."

Mark groaned. His suffering was useless. One way or another, they would order events to their will. Even so, he would keep faith with her. "I did not lie with the Lady."

I

The stick twisted. Mark screamed. And suddenly his resolution broke. "I will sign!"

"Not so fast, Mark. We must know about the others. Did not Sir Francis Weston lie with her also? And Henry Norris? And William Berenton?"

"Aye," Mark groaned. "All of them."

"And Lord Rochford?"

Rochford! Her own brother! She was doomed, even more surely than he himself was, but even so, he could not allow this final befoulment of her name, this charge of incest. "No! Not Rochford."

The stick twisted, twice. Mark screamed again. With blood and tears running down his face, he said, "Aye, Rochford too."

1

JUDITH DUNNE had come to the Tower that bright June afternoon for two reasons. First, she had a few hours to kill. Second, that complex of ancient structures and fairly modern ones set around cobbled courtyards and small stretches of lawn was one of her favorite spots in London. With its much-restored round towers of white or honey-colored stone, its pennants rippling in the breeze, its Yeoman Warders in Tudor dress, it seemed to her light-heartedly false, like a stage set for a musical comedy version of *Ivanhoe*.

Then, moving with a group of camera-hung tourists across Tower Green, she received a jarring reminder that however carefree its present-day atmosphere, real cries of despair and agony had echoed through those round towers, and real blood had soaked wooden scaffolds here under the open sky. Just ahead, surrounded by a low metal railing, was a small area paved with brick. Judith did not need to read the words on a nearby signboard. She knew from former visits that it bore the names of six persons who had knelt to the headsman at this spot, including Anne Boleyn.

Judith felt an impulse to cross her arms in front of her, as if under the onslaught of a sudden cold wind. It was not the thought of Anne Boleyn, baring "such a little neck" to the swordsman that spring morning four and a half centuries ago, which chilled Judith. It was the thought of a young woman who had died less than a year ago in a London suburb, her spinal cord severed, not by a sword of finest Toledo steel, but by some unknown weapon, perhaps a kitchen cleaver—

"Stop it," she commanded herself. Turning away from the railed enclosure, she started back toward the entrance to the Tower. Only this morning a 747 had returned her to London after her long, unhappy winter in New York. If she intended to stay here all summer, actually living in that little carriage-house apartment so close to that big main house where it had happened, then she must stop thinking about Cecily's death.

"Miss Dunne?"

Startled, she halted and looked up at the tall young man beside her. He was one of those dark Englishmen whose looks hint that their ancestors might have included some sailor or soldier washed ashore from the wrecked Spanish Armada. Dark hair, loosely waving and worn rather long in back. Brown eyes—the eyes of a scholar, thoughtful and somewhat tired looking. An olive-skinned face with a straight nose and a full lower lip. His brown corduroy jacket and gray flannel trousers, in an era when most men under thirty wore denims or chinos for almost every occasion, struck her as pleasantly traditional.

Aware that they knew each other, and yet unable to place him, Judith smiled uncertainly. He said, "Kyle Hodge. Last summer. Hampton Court Palace."

Of course! Kyle Hodge, teacher of history in a boys' school. Kyle Hodge, whose mother, once a nannie in the household of a relative of the Queen, had been rewarded with one of the government-subsidized apartments inside Hampton Court's ancient walls. What were they called, those living quarters which the Queen had the

4

right to bestow in return for "special services to the Crown"? The phrase came back to Judith. Grace-and-favor apartments. Judith also recalled how last summer, as she toiled over her drawing board in some echoing stone gallery or long-empty room at the palace, Kyle sometimes had stopped beside her to make a friendly comment about her work.

Judith said, "Forgive me. I knew that I knew you. But when I see people where I'm not used to seeing them, it's hard sometimes for me to place them."

"Perfectly all right." His East Anglian accent made the last word sound almost like "raught." He went on, "I know what you mean about seeing people out of context. When I saw you a moment ago I didn't know immediately who you were. In fact, for a second or two—"

Abruptly he broke off. She said, "For a second or two you thought I was Cecily."

He nodded. True, the American girl looking up at him wore her dark hair longer than Cecily had. In contrast to the chiseled perfection of Cecily's face, Judith's features were softer and more rounded. And her eyes were a very different shade of brown. Cecily's had been almost black. The American girl's were nearly a golden brown, like sunlit brook water running over autumn leaves. Nevertheless, the resemblance between Judith and her dead English cousin was remarkable.

He asked, "When did you return to London?"

"This morning. I took a Pan Am night flight from New York."

"How long will you be here?"

"All summer. You see, I'm going to illustrate another book for teenagers about Hampton Court Palace. Not about the Tudors this time. This one will be about the Stuart monarchs who lived there."

"Is the book by the same author as the one you illus-

5

trated last summer?" She nodded. "Didn't you say he was a friend of yours?"

"Yes." But the truth was that from her first meeting with Barney Wallace, she had thought of him as much more than a friend.

Kyle said, "Would you like a cup of tea?"

She hesitated only a moment. She liked this un-English looking young Englishman, liked him especially, because she knew, from comments he'd made the previous summer, that underneath his quiet, pleasant exterior he felt an enduring anger with some of the world's inequities. His indignation, she sensed, was less on his own behalf than that of his servant-class mother.

"Yes," Judith said, "I would like that very much."

A few minutes later, in the noisy self-service restaurant just inside the Tower's high stone walls, they smiled at each other across thick mugs of tea. He asked, "Do you have a place to stay?"

After a moment she answered, "Yes, the same place where I stayed last summer."

He was unable to keep surprise out of his voice. "You mean that carriage-house apartment behind the Grenville house?"

"Yes. Cecily's husband inherited the property, of course. But she specified in her will that I was to have the use of the carriage-house apartment whenever I chose to. Her lawyer wrote and told me so after her will was probated last winter."

He said tentatively, "I should think, after the shock of your cousin's death—"

"Yes, it was a shock." Aside from the horror, she had felt incredulity. How could it be that Cecily Grenville—rich, beautiful, self-assured Cecily—should fall victim to an anonymous murderer, like some obscure woman knifed by a mugger in a New York tenement hallway?

6

"But she left the use of the apartment to me," she went on, "and it would seem—oh, rather ungrateful not to use the place, now that I need it." Although usually self-centered, Cecily had been subject to fits of generosity. It must have been at such a moment, Judith reflected, that she had added that clause to her will. Or had she done it to annoy her husband? Judith could imagine her, sometime last summer, showing the new clause to Steven, thus reminding him afresh that the money and property were hers to dispose of as she wished.

Kyle lifted the tea bag from his mug and placed it in the saucer. A shock, Judith had said. To him the news of Cecily Grenville's death had been not just a shock, but a shattering blow from which, almost a year later, he had not yet recovered. He remembered waking late that morning last August in his room in his Aunt Sara's house in Barnbridge Wells, eighty miles northeast of London. He'd switched on the wireless on the stand beside his bed. A Rolling Stones recording had given way to the ten A.M. news. Cecily Lowery Grenville, sole heir of the late Alfred Lowery, publisher of newspapers devoted to horse racing, had been found murdered in the bedroom of her house near Hampton Court Village.

He had stared up at the ceiling, numb with disbelief. Only the night before in the wide bed in her bedroom —a large and rather tasteless room, like all the others in that house—he had made love to her. And although he had parted from her in anger and humiliation, he had a vivid memory of the joy, almost the awe, his possession of that cool-eyed, beautiful creature had brought him. It had been his first possession of her. And now he knew it would be his last.

He had felt an impulse to drive back to Hampton Court Village and learn all that he could about Cecily's death. On the other hand he felt reluctant to retrace the miles he had driven the night before, throbbing with rage. And so he had lingered on most of that day in the neat house that was as familiar to him as his mother's apartment at Hampton Court.

In mid-afternoon he had hurried down to the village station to buy one of the newspapers brought in on the three o'clock train. According to the paper it was Steven Grenville, returning to his home after midnight, who had discovered his wife's body. Presumably asleep, she had been lying in her bed on her stomach, left hand resting on the pillow, when someone had struck her with some sharp instrument across the back of the neck, severing the spinal cord.

No valuables were missing, a fact that had caused the police to rule out robbery as a motive, and no murder weapon had been found. But the Grenville cook, who like the two other servants came in each morning and went home at night, had stated that a cleaver was missing from a kitchen drawer. Perhaps it had been the weapon, and perhaps the murderer had taken it away with him.

Soon after reading the newspaper's account Kyle had driven back to his mother's Hampton Court apartment. Neither that evening nor at any time afterward had the police questioned him, although they interviewed dozens of Cecily's friends and acquaintances, ranging from rock musicians to Chelsea boutique owners to some of the more rakish members of the peerage. Apparently it never occurred to anyone that the beautiful Mrs. Grenville might have been intimate even briefly with an obscure history teacher, spending his summer with his ex-nursemaid mother in one of those Crown-subsidized apartments at Hampton Court Palace.

More than once he had felt that he should tell the police that, except for her murderer, he was probably the last person who saw Cecily Grenville alive. But he could think of no way in which that would help them find her killer. And he shrank from the thought that under police questioning he might repeat the words she had said to him—words that had sent him from her house to the nearest pub where, eventually, he had decided that he could not stay anywhere near Cecily Grenville for the rest of that night.

Now, still looking down at his tea mug, he wondered for perhaps the hundredth time if Cecily's husband had killed her. Oh, he had an ironclad alibi for that night. At the time of her death he had been twenty miles away and in the company of scores of people who knew him. But it would not be the first time that a man had given himself an unassailable alibi while a hired killer did his work for him.

Judith said, almost as if her thoughts had followed his own, "Do you know if Steven Grenville still lives in the main house?"

"I don't think so. I think he rented a flat somewhere near his office on the high street in Hampton Court Village. The last I heard, the house was empty." He paused. "Does Grenville know you're here?"

"Yes. Before I left New York I telephoned him. He said that if I dropped by his office at five this afternoon he would turn over the key of the carriage-house apartment to me." Her brown eyes looked straight into Kyle's. "I suppose you think it is callous of me to choose to spend the summer within a couple of hundred feet of where Cecily—died."

He looked at the wide-spaced eyes, the slightly tilted nose, the full, sensitive mouth. He smiled. "I don't think you could be callous if you tried."

"Thank you. The truth is that not having to pay rent will be important to me. My financial situation isn't of the soundest."

Her unhappiness over Barney Wallace last winter had affected her work. Three times she had accepted publishers' invitations to submit sample illustrations for children's books, only to be told that the drawings lacked the originality and charm they had come to expect from Judith Dunne. She had been about to give up, go back to Edmonton, Kentucky, and work in her father's real estate office. Then one night the phone rang. She heard Barney's familiar voice, holding a tentative, almost humble note that was not at all familiar. After the way he'd behaved, he said, he wouldn't blame her for turning him down cold. Still, would she possibly consider illustrating the new book he was writing, another one about Hampton Court? He'd heard, via the grapevine, that in her cousin's will she had been left free use of the apartment she'd occupied the previous summer, so if by any chance she would consider—

Kyle Hodge thought, watching her, "She's been hurt, and not just financially." Had some man let her down? Possibly, although it was hard to imagine a man discarding such a pretty and thoroughly nice girl. From the expression that had flitted across her face when he asked about the authorship of the new book she was to illustrate, he rather thought that if some man had hurt her it might be that writing chap. And yet she was illustrating another book of his. Why? Because she needed the money? Or because, in spite of whatever hurt he had dealt her, she still loved him? Yes, he thought wryly, considering the tendency of human beings to want the very people who were the least good for them, that second explanation might be the real one.

Judith said, "Are you still teaching at that boys' school near Sheffield?"

"No. I left there halfway through the spring term. In the fall I'll join the staff of a school in Nottingham."

He could tell she was wondering whether he had left his former post voluntarily or had been sacked. She was too polite, though, to ask. Instead she said, "And how about this summer? Are you staying with your mother again?"

"Yes."

Judith felt a little puzzled by that, just as she had the previous summer. Kyle Hodge did not strike her as a mama's boy. Perhaps it was not any sort of emotional dependency that caused him each summer to share his mother's apartment overlooking Base Court, the ancient palace's largest courtyard. Perhaps it was a desire to assuage her loneliness. Because surely she must be lonely. About all she had in common with most of the other grace-and-favor tenants was her sex and her widowhood. She was a retired nannie. The other women, many of them titled, were widows of admirals and generals and cabinet members.

Judith looked at her watch. "Oh, lord! Almost three. And I'm supposed to pick up that apartment key from Steven Grenville at five."

"Are you driving down to Hampton Court?"

"No. I'll have to rent a car later on, but I haven't done so yet."

"I'd be glad to drive you, but in half an hour I'm to meet an old school friend at a pub near St. Paul's."

"No matter. I'll take the red bus from here to Victoria bus station, pick up my suitcase there, and then catch a green country bus to Hampton Court."

"I'll go out to the bus stop with you."

They walked out into the June sunshine and, turning right, moved against the tide of sightseers streaming through the entrance gate in the honey-colored stone wall. Judith said, "By the way, what were you doing here today? I thought that the English seldom came to places like the Tower of London, just the way native New Yorkers almost never visit Grant's Tomb."

When he didn't answer, she looked up at him. He said quickly, "After all, I'm a history teacher. I thought that the boys in my classes next fall might like a firsthand account of what the Tower of London looks like."

Now why, she wondered, should a simple question like that have upset him. She did not know. But from his constrained tone and the uncomfortable look on his sensitive face she knew that it had.

2

THE GREEN COUNTRY BUS with its cargo of bundle-laden shoppers moved past Kensington Gardens, affording a distant glimpse of the palace where Queen Victoria once lived blissfully with her Albert, and where, much later, Princess Margaret had lived less amicably with Lord Snowdon. It moved past the trendy boutiques on Kensington High Street. Then, gradually, elegance gave way to the noise and bustle of lower middle-class Hammersmith.

Although she stared out the window, Judith did not really see the shop fronts plastered with sale signs, or the sidewalk counters piled high with jeans and tee-shirts. She was thinking of herself and Cecily, and of how strange it was that the two of them—one growing up in a small Kentucky town, the other in London—should be first cousins. In fact they were even closer, biologically speaking, than most first cousins because their mothers, the pretty Gale sisters of Edmonton, Kentucky, had been identical twins.

It was on a trip through the Kentucky horse country that a Londoner named Alfred Lowery had met the Gale twins. Joyce Gale, who became Judith's mother, was already married to a real estate agent named Dunne, but Julia Gale was available. The young Englishman was what the British call an oddsmaker, and the Americans call a bookie. Consequently Mr. and Mrs. Gale and their daughter Joyce had all opposed Julia's interest in him. Nevertheless, Julia and Alfred had eloped to New York, married there, and flown to London.

A year later, soon after the birth of his daughter Cecily, Alfred Lowery had scraped together enough money to start publishing *The Lowery Racing News*. Within five years his paper was on sale at newsstands from Inverness to Brighton, and he was on his way to amassing his first million pounds.

Growing up in that small Kentucky town with her parents and grandparents, Judith speculated often about her English cousin, and hoped for a visit from her. But apparently the feeling between Judith's grandparents and her mother on the one hand, and runaway Julia and her English husband on the other, remained too bitter to permit more than an occasional exchange of stiffly polite letters. When Judith was twenty, one such letter announced that Cecily had married an architect named Steven Grenville.

During Judith's last year as an art major at a small Kentucky college, her grandmother Gale had died, leaving her a small legacy. After graduating, Judith had used the money to go to New York and begin a career as an illustrator, first for a magazine and later for various book publishers. She had been in New York almost two years when her mother telephoned one night, her voice hushed with shock. Julia Gale Lowery and her husband were dead. Guests aboard a yacht owned by a Greek shipping magnate, they and ten others had been lost when the vessel capsized off the Canary Islands in a storm.

As soon as her mother had hung up, Judith wrote a letter of condolence addressed to Mrs. Steven Grenville,

The Columns, near Hampton Court Village, Middlesex, England. Cecily's reply, scrawled in extravagantly large handwriting on thick cream-colored notepaper, had struck Judith as strange indeed. Cecily had written:

> Yes, I miss Mum and Daddy, but there are consolations. I mean, if one has to die, what better way to go than aboard a billionaire's yacht?
>
> Why don't you pop over here for a visit, Cousin Judith? Who knows, you and I might hit it off very well. You might even like my husband, although I often doubt that I do. It's strange to fall in love with a man because he reminds you of Steve McQueen, and then find yourself married to someone like that Leslie Howard character in *Gone With the Wind*.
>
> Do think about coming.
>
> $\hspace{4cm}$ *À bientôt,*
> $\hspace{4cm}$ Cee-cee.

That letter had made Judith less eager to see her cousin. But at a publisher's cocktail party one April afternoon she had met Barney Wallace. Sturdy and wide-shouldered, with curly brown hair, blue eyes, and a crooked grin, he looked more like a boxer than a writer of teenager's books. As they stood, drinks in hand, at the window of the big, noisy room overlooking Central Park West, Barney said, "I loved your illustrations for that juvenile about Bonnie Prince Charlie. How's that book doing, by the way?"

"Quite well."

"I shouldn't wonder. After all these juvenile books about street gangs, divorcing parents, and venereal disease, I imagine the kids find a rousing historical a relief. Anyway, I'm going to gamble on it. The book I'm writing now is about Hampton Court Palace during the days of the Tudor monarchs."

"Is Hampton Court Palace near the village of Hampton Court?"

"Of course. There was a village outside the palace walls even before Henry the Eighth blackjacked poor old Cardinal Wolsey into giving him the place. Why do you ask?"

"Because I have a cousin who lives near the village of Hampton Court."

Head on one side, Barney sloshed his vodka-and-orange-juice around in its glass. "I've got an idea. While I'm writing the last chapters, why don't you go over there, stay with your cousin, and do the illustrations for my book? I'm sure my publisher can arrange matters with the office of the Lord Chamberlain, or whoever, so that you can set up your easel at various spots in the palace."

They had gone to dinner at a small French restaurant on East Eighty-sixth Street. Before the meal was over, Judith knew that in a few weeks she would go to Hampton Court. In fact, already she was sufficiently smitten with him that she might have agreed to go to Lapland to illustrate a book about reindeer-herding.

That night she wrote to Cecily. Her cousin's airmailed reply, when it finally arrived more than two weeks later, was cordial.

You can have your own apartment above the old carriage house. The people from whom Daddy bought this place—he gave it to me just before I married Steven, you know—used the apartment as servants' quarters, but Steven and I don't have live-in help. Anyway, I hear that quiet and privacy is very important to you creative types. And you will be far enough away from the main house that you won't hear much even if some of my rocker

16

friends are giving a private concert in my living room.

Sorry not to have answered sooner, but we've had a bit of an upset here. A girl named Annette Swayle was killed here in the village two weeks ago. They found her knifed to death in the bus-stop shelter right across the road from Hampton Court Palace. She worked for us whenever we needed extra help. In fact, Steven had given her a lift home only a few hours before her body was found, and so as you can imagine the police were asking a lot of questions. They've stopped bothering us now, even though as far as I know the poor twerps still don't have a clue as to who killed her.

Anyway, do please come.

Love,
Cee-cee.

It took another two weeks for Barney's publishers to draw up Judith's contract and to obtain official permission for her to use parts of the palace and its grounds in her sketches. By that time she and Barney were bound together by far more than a publisher's contract, a happy state of affairs which she hoped would become permanent.

Now, as the country bus carried her along a road separated from the Thames by a sloping green embankment, she thought of the May night more than a year in the past when Barney had taken her to Kennedy Airport and kissed her goodbye. All through the flight over the black Atlantic, visible now and then through rifts in the clouds, she had been too absorbed in her thoughts—of the strange country toward which she was traveling at six hundred miles an hour, of Barney, and of how blissful it would be to return to him at the end of the summer —that she didn't even try to sleep.

Around eight the next morning the plane had descended through a thick gray smother to Heathrow Airport. The calendar said spring but the English temperature said winter. As the plane taxied through the murky light toward the arrivals building, Judith saw long grass at the airstrip's edge blown flat by the wind. And when she emerged from the customs area she saw that many of the people waiting to greet the plane's passengers wore heavy clothing. Among them was a tall, dark-haired girl in faded jeans and a tee-shirt, topped by an ankle-length red fox coat that must have cost seven thousand dollars. Beside her stood an even taller blond man with a thin, high-cheekboned face who appeared to be in his early thirties, and who wore dark gray trousers and a tweed jacket.

Even if she had not seen a clipping of Cecily's bridal photograph from the London *Times,* Judith would have known that the tall girl was her cousin. We look a lot alike, Judith thought, except that she's beautiful, really beautiful.

Cecily and the blond man were approaching. "You're Judith, aren't you? Of course you are." She bent and kissed Judith's cheek. "And this is my husband, Steven."

"How do you do?" His smile barely touched his lips, and did not appear in his gray eyes at all.

Cecily smiled up at her husband. "She looks like me, doesn't she? Except nicer, of course. In fact, she looks like the sort of girl you wish I were, doesn't she, Stevie darling?"

He said evenly, "Don't start that sort of thing. Can't you realize she must be tired?"

Cecily laughed. "What a fake! You're not concerned about her being tired. You're just afraid I'll embarrass you." She hooked her arm through Judith's. "Come on. We'll collect your luggage."

Out in the parking lot about twenty minutes later they stopped beside a dark green Mercedes. Steven Grenville opened the door for Judith to get into the back seat, placed her large suitcase in the boot, and then turned to his wife. "Do you want to ride in the back seat with your cousin?"

"Nice try, Steven. But I intend to drive. You sit in the back if you like."

Judith saw a muscle leap along his jaw. "You're not a heavy-traffic driver. You nearly ran into a lorry on the way here. Do you want to smash up a brand-new car?"

"Not particularly." She opened the door on the driver's side and got behind the wheel. "But if I do, I can afford another one."

Not answering, he got into the car beside her.

As Cecily started the engine, she looked into the rear view mirror and smiled at Judith. "Don't be nervous about my driving. I did not almost hit a lorry. Steven says that sort of thing because he doesn't like me to drive when he's in the car." She backed and then turned toward the car park exit. Beside her her husband sat motionless, shoulders rigid. "I think he feels it has an emasculating effect. I tell him that a man sure of his masculinity wouldn't mind if his wife drives.

"Sorry!" she said, a moment later, looking into the rear view mirror. "I've embarrassed you, haven't I, Judith? Well, from now on I'll just let you look at the scenery. I'm afraid it won't be very spectacular. We're bypassing London and taking the direct route to Hampton Court."

Cecily had been right about the scenery. It consisted of flat stretches of uncultivated land between groups of new-looking houses. But Judith was grateful that Cecily confined herself to comments about the landscape, such as it was, and about the heavy traffic. After a while Cecily's words seemed to fade out. Judith leaned back in one corner of the seat and closed her eyes.

"—wall around Bushey Park, part of the Hampton

Court Palace grounds. Lots of tame deer inside there. There always have been, for hundreds of years." With a start Judith came awake. "That sour-faced Scotsman, James the First, so somebody told me," Cecily went on, "used to hide behind trees and take pot shots at them. No one's allowed to shoot them these days, of course."

Wide awake now, Judith saw that they had left the motorway and were on a narrower road that ran past a high wall of ancient-looking red brick. Her pulses quickened. So there it was, somewhere beyond that brick wall, that place she had read so much about ever since she had met Barney. Hampton Court Palace, originally built by a butcher's son who had become a Cardinal and the richest man in England. Hampton Court Palace, where an aging Queen Catherine of Aragon waged a lonely fight against a King Henry determined to divorce her, and where the ghost of another Queen Catherine was still said to run shrieking along the Haunted Corridor, hoping to find that same King Henry and plead with him to spare her life.

Now, on this warm June afternoon more than a year later, Judith realized that the green bus was passing that same spot along the Bushey Park wall. The bus turned the corner and moved past the wide entrance gate set in the wall. She caught a glimpse up the long drive of the palace's high Tudor façade, all red brick and leaded windows and twisted stone chimneys, before the bus continued on across the bridge spanning the Thames and stopped in front of the Hampton Court railroad station. Suitcase in hand, she crossed the side road and then moved down the village's curving high street, past the estate agents' offices and tearooms and antique shops. As she neared Steven Grenville's office she was aware, not of fear exactly, but a distinct uneasiness. From the first Cecily's husband, with his aloof gray eyes and bony face, had made her feel ill at ease. But there was no reason to be afraid of him. No matter how quarrelsome his relations with Cecily, he could not have been the one who killed her. At least the police, apparently, were satisfied of his innocence. As always in such cases, they had considered the husband the prime suspect until they had investigated his alibi. It had held up. Until almost midnight of the night of his wife's death he had been twenty miles away at a dinner in London of the Architectural Society, never out of sight for more than a few minutes of many people who knew him.

Here was the place, a modern one-story building of white brick. An engraved brass plate beside the door read, "Steven Grenville, Architect." For the first time, Judith wondered why the plate did not also say, "By Royal Appointment." Well, perhaps he was not entitled to style himself in that way, even though he was the architect who had to approve even the smallest of the repairs and alterations at Hampton Court Palace, as well as consult with architects in charge of repairs at other Royal Monuments.

She opened the door and stepped into a small outer office. A gray-haired woman looked up, smiling, from her desk. "Welcome back, Miss Dunne."

"Thank you, Miss Claverly. It's good to be back." Or it would be if she found that she did not mind staying in that carriage-house apartment. She had told herself in New York that she would not mind. But now that she was within five miles of that apartment and of the house where Cecily had died, she was not so sure.

"Mr. Grenville asked me to rent a car for you," Miss Claverly said. "It's across the street, a blue Volvo. I put some groceries in the boot, staples plus sausages and a few tinned things. Oh, and I had the apartment telephone hooked up."

"Thank you so very much, especially for the groceries." Cooking dinner on the apartment's small gas stove tonight, as she had most nights the previous summer, might make her feel at home again. "I'll pay you what I owe you after I've seen Mr. Grenville. Is he—"

"He's expecting you. Go right in."

She opened a door into a much larger room, filled with the mingled light of late afternoon coming through the windows and the fluorescent glare beating down from ceiling tubes. Steven Grenville, standing at a long, high table, palms resting on an outspread blueprint, straightened up and turned to her. "Hello, Judith." As when they had first met, his brief smile did not warm his eyes.

"Hello, Steven. Thank you for asking Miss Claverly to rent a car for me."

"Not at all."

She realized then that probably he had wanted her to have the car from the first so that she would not expect him to drive her out to The Columns. She said, "You're not living in the main house, are you?"

He looked at her coolly. "No, I have a flat here in the village. An estate agent is trying to find a tenant for the house."

She had something to say to him. Might as well get it over with right at the start. "I hope you don't mind Cecily's leaving me the use of that apartment. I had no idea she was going to do so."

"Why should I mind? That old carriage house has never been used as a garage." Sometime not long after the turn of the century, a former owner had added a garage at right angles to the house's rear wall. "And the space above the carriage house isn't needed. As a matter of fact, there is far more space in the main house than most people want these days.

"And anyway," he went on, in that same even voice,

"I could have had that clause in my wife's will in-validated, if I had cared to go to the trouble."

The letter from the lawyer handling Cecily's estate had told her as much. The clause would hold up, the lawyer had written, as long as the new owner, Steven Grenville, did not challenge it. Still, it annoyed her that Steven should stress that it was only by his sufferance that the place would be hers this summer.

She said, in a voice as cool as his own, "Thank you for your generosity. May I have the keys now?"

"Miss Claverly has them."

Judith realized that he wanted to keep contact be-tween them at a minimum. Perhaps he had hoped that she would be late this afternoon, thus giving him an excuse to leave his office before she arrived. Why? Because he disliked her? Or because she reminded him of his dead wife? "Very well. Good afternoon," she said, and walked out.

3

AFTER INSPECTING the groceries Miss Claverly had placed in the rented Volvo, Judith decided to supplement them with eggs, milk, and lettuce. She drove down the high street to a small greengrocers' and went inside.

As she emerged from the shop and moved across the sidewalk toward the car, a green Ferrari coming down the street pulled into the curb a few feet ahead of the Volvo and stopped. By the time she had placed her purchases beside the other groceries in the boot and walked back to the car's right-hand door, the Ferrari's driver was moving toward her along the sidewalk. The way he walked reminded Judith of the one time she had seen a television performance of his. In green face paint, a Medusa headdress of green plastic snakes, and a green satin jumpsuit so tight that it too looked painted on, he had moved across the stage with that same lithe prowl, bringing excited screams from his mainly adolescent audience. Today he wore brown cowboy boots and pants and a fringed jacket of beige buckskin. A Stetson of the same pale color shadowed his sharp-featured face. His name was Zack Reeve, and he was organizer and lead guitarist of a rock group called the Living Nightmares.

He said, not at all unpleasantly, "Hello, Snow White." He had dubbed her that when, during one of Cecily's parties, she had turned down his suggestion that they retire to one of the upstairs bedrooms. "What are you doing back on this side of the Atlantic, luv? Going to draw pictures for another kiddie book?"

"Yes." Then, to forestall a question as to where she was staying: "What are you doing in Hampton Court Village?"

He grinned the wide, wolfish grin which showed his pointed incisors and which, for some reason inexplicable to adults, always sent his youngest fans into paroxysms of delight. "I'm not revisiting the scene of the crime, if that's what you're thinking, luv."

"Now why should I think that?"

He shrugged. "No real reason. After all, I was more than a hundred miles away from here, on a stage in Liverpool with a couple of thousand people looking at me, the night somebody did poor Cee-cee in. But I thought you might wonder why I'm back here, seeing that she isn't around to throw those parties my mates and I used to go to." When she said nothing, he went on, "I'm here looking for ideas for the Nightmares' new album. Ideas for the background of the cover photograph, I mean."

It struck her that the vicinity of Hampton Court Palace was one of the last places where a grotesquely costumed group of rockers might find a suitable background for an album cover photograph. But because she wanted to cut the conversation short she did not say so. Instead she got into the driver's seat and closed the door. "Nice to have seen you, Zack."

"Not so fast." He crossed his arms on the car's window ledge and peered in at her. "Where are you staying?" When she was slow in answering he grinned and said, "It won't be hard for me to find out, you know."

"There would be no point in your doing that." She tried to keep her voice from being unfriendly. True, she found him not in the least attractive. But he hadn't become snide and nasty that time she had turned him down, and she had appreciated that.

"You're sure there'd be no point? You might like me better if we spent a little time alone."

"Please, Zack. I hear that whenever you go on tour there are hordes of girls trying to break down your dressing room door. So why should you bother with me?"

"A challenge, luv. The one who gets away is always a challenge. But we'll leave it for now." He stepped back from the car. "*Ciao,* as Cee-cee used to say."

"Goodbye, Zack."

She drove on down the high street and then turned to her left along a narrow, tree-bordered road now deep in late-afternoon shadow. For the first half-mile there were a few scattered houses set well back from the road. After that there were only open fields beyond the trees until, about five miles from the village, she saw a corner of The Columns' red brick wall up ahead on the left-hand side of the road. She stopped the car on the grassy verge, got out, and unlocked the wrought-iron gates with the heavy key Miss Claverly had given her. She drove through. As she got out again to relock the gate, she reflected that neither the locked gate nor the five-foot wall could protect the property from a determined intruder. Any reasonably fit person of either sex could scale the wall. But at least the lock kept out the idly curious who, seeing through the wrought-iron gate that the lawn was unmowed and that window draperies were drawn, might have driven in for a closer look at an obviously empty house.

When she had relocked the gate she herself turned to gaze at the house. Like the five-hundred-year-old palace only a few miles away, The Columns had been built of red brick. There the resemblance ended. The house, built around 1895, was fake Georgian. From its white, semicircular portico rose the wooden columns, also white, which gave the house its name. The reddish-yellow light of the declining sun glittered in its attic windows although the ground-floor windows, protected by tall curved grilles of wrought iron, were already in shadow.

Judith reflected that if the Victorian builders had followed the mode of their day—cupolas and bay windows and panes of colored glass set into windows and doors—the house might have had more character. As it was, they had produced a poor imitation of the sort of house built a hundred years before their time. To Judith it seemed that there was something sad and lost about that house. It was neither small and friendly nor, despite its two stories and an attic, truly large and impressive. And it had no roots in its own time.

But perhaps that was why Cecily had felt drawn to the house. She herself seemed a rootless person, much too rich to be a part of the lower class from which her father, a navvy's son, had sprung, but with no desire to become an accepted member of the upper classes. In fact, Judith felt, that had been one of the nice things about her cousin. Cecily had not cared whether the names of someone's parents appeared in Burke's *Peerage* or on the Birmingham welfare roles. All she asked of people was that she find them amusing, and that they have enough money, however acquired, to play roulette and blackjack in London gambling clubs all night, and to accompany her to the Greek islands or Marrakech whenever she wanted to go there. In fact, sometimes she had paid the plane fares of temporarily strapped friends.

Judith recalled how once last summer Cecily had talked of how she had acquired The Columns. "I told Daddy that I wanted to marry this architect who had to

27

be at Hampton Court Palace a lot, and that I'd seen a house for sale not far from there. Daddy bought the place all right, but he put it in my name, not mine and Steven's." She had given a wry laugh. "You see, Daddy was brighter than me. He could tell we were not going to jog contentedly through the years, like Darby and Joan."

Now, standing beside her rented car, Judith realized that the house, though unoccupied, was not empty of furniture. Through a slit between the drawn draperies at a ground-floor window she could make out the back of a sofa upholstered in some dark material—dark red velvet if she remembered correctly. She got into the car, drove it back along the northern wall of the house and past the back lawn with the one-story attached garage built along its southern edge. She stopped at the foot of wooden steps leading up the side of the old brick carriage house to the door of the apartment above.

She found the silent, familiar rooms neat but airless. Opening windows as she went, she moved into the tiny kitchen just off the short entrance hall and then along the hall to the living room and the bedroom beyond. The bed was made up with sheet and blanket and a blue cotton spread. In the small bathroom with its plain white fixtures, light blue hand towels and bath towels hung from rods. Miss Claverly's doing, undoubtedly. And she must have done it on her own initiative. Steven Grenville, wanting only to keep a distance between himself and his dead wife's cousin, would never have asked his secretary to give the apartment a welcoming air.

She unpacked her large suitcase, stowing clothes away in the small closet and chest of drawers, and then changed from her lightweight green pantsuit to jeans and a white cotton shirt. In the living room with its braided gray and blue rug, its sofa and wing chair upholstered in glazed floral print with draperies to match, she drew a straight chair up to a small gateleg table beside the window. She went into the kitchen, returned with a white ironstone plate and silver and a place mat, and set the table.

Twenty minutes later she carried from the kitchen the cheese omelet and green salad she had prepared. Although it was well past nine, enough daylight lingered so that she did not have to turn on the lamp. As she ate, she deliberately glanced now and then out across the unmowed grass to the rear wall of the main house. She had decided that since she was to stay here all summer it would be useless to try to ignore the nearness of that house, and of the window to that second-floor corner room where her self-willed and yet in many ways generous cousin had died.

Judith had occupied this apartment less than a week the previous summer when she concluded that Cecily and Steven's marriage was hopelessly bad. She'd reached that belief after the one and only occasion when she had spent an evening out with the Grenvilles. First they had gone to a restaurant in the village which, according to the bronze plaque beside its entrance, occupied the site where a tavern had stood in the days of Henry the Eighth. Afterward they had driven through the night to the most fashionable of London's discothèques. Throughout the evening Cecily had made barbed comments to and about Steven. He had received most of her remarks in stony silence, although now and then he'd responded with a hostility that matched her own. At the discothèque, where Cecily had seemed to know everyone and where she and Judith both had danced with at least a dozen partners, Steven had sat drink in hand at a table, looking at the dancers with a cold amusement which suggested that he was not just a decade older than most of them, but several decades.

At three in the morning they drove home, with Steven sitting grimly silent behind the wheel, and his wife, apparently with her fund of malice temporarily exhausted, curled up in the opposite corner of the seat. In the back seat, Judith decided that she would not go out with them again.

She did not. And she went to only two of the frequent and noisy parties that Cecily gave in the main house. It was not just that Judith was made uneasy by the guests who took cocaine at about ten dollars a sniff, and the once seductive but now blowsy British film star who was subject to crying jags, and the rock musicians, not only Zack Reeve and his "mates," but another group who wore boots with five-inch-thick soles and whose speech, filled with rocker slang and delivered in a Lancashire accent, was as incomprehensible to her as if they had been speaking Bantu. No, for her the most unpleasant moment of those parties was when Steven had come home from God only knew where and, before going upstairs, had paused for a moment in the living room doorway, his face holding a cold disgust. Herself the product of a happy marriage, and confident that someday she and Barney would marry with equal success, Judith felt repelled by the ugly relationship that the Grenvilles' had become. And so, pleading that she had work to do, she begged off from further invitations to attend Cecily's parties, or to join her cousin and her husband on the rare occasions when they went out together. Instead she spent nearly all of her evenings in her apartment, studying the sketch she had worked on that day—a sketch of Catherine of Aragon staring tragic-faced through a casement window of the palace, or her successor Anne Boleyn seated at her embroidery frame, or King Henry in the palace's roofed tennis court, lofting the ball across the net while his subjects in the viewing balcony applauded rapturously.

But no matter how successfully she avoided seeing the Grenvilles together, she could not help hearing them. She recalled one night in particular when loud, angry voices had come from the window of what she knew was Cecily's room. Suddenly Judith heard her cousin cry out.

The next morning as she drove her rented car—not a Volvo that previous summer, but an English Ford—down the road toward the village, she saw Cecily ahead of her in the little red MG she often used for solitary drives. Speeding up, Judith drew alongside the smaller car and gestured for her cousin to pull over to the side of the road. When both cars had stopped Judith walked back through the tall roadside grass to Cecily.

"Are you all right? I mean, last night I heard some sort of—row."

For answer Cecily pushed her dark glasses to the top of her head. Her left eye, swollen almost shut, was surrounded by a mass of purple flesh.

Shocked into bluntness, Judith said, "You've got to get a divorce. You two can't go on like this."

Cecily had sighed. "I suppose so. But I hate the thought of lawyers and a property settlement and the whole bit."

"Property settlement?"

"Of course. If Steven makes it easy for me to divorce him, shouldn't I settle some money on him?" Her tone was lightly satirical. "After all, didn't he give me the best two years of his life?"

Judith tried to keep the distaste out of her voice. "Well, of course that's up to you two. I'd better get to work now."

She started to turn away. "Wait!" Cecily said. When Judith turned back the English girl reached into the

MG's glove compartment, took out a small handgun, and offered it, butt-end first, to her cousin.

Shrinking back, Judith said, "What's that?"

"A gun, of course. An automatic to be exact. I want to give it to you."

"But I don't want—"

"Please!" Cecily rested the gun on the car door's ledge. "It can't hurt you. The safety's on. Keep it in your car today and then when you come back to the apartment put it in a drawer. After all, you're alone there. It might be a good idea for you to have a gun."

"But why—"

"Why do I want to get rid of it? Because last night, if I could have remembered quickly what drawer I'd put it in, I might have used it on Steven. This morning I decided I'd better—just throw it away someplace. But if I go on thinking about this black eye, I might decide to keep it after all. So you take it. I'll come to your apartment after dinner and show you how to load and unload it."

Cecily was smiling, but nevertheless there was frightened appeal in her bruised face. Judith thought, feeling sick, she really is afraid of what she might do. Aloud she said, "All right." Gingerly she took the gun, carried it to her car, and put it in the glove compartment. Before stepping on the starter, she looked in the rear view mirror. Cecily still sat behind the wheel of her motionless car. She had lowered her dark glasses, hiding the bruise. But all the rest of the way to the village, Judith kept remembering that black eye, and Cecily's talk of settling money on Steven.

As it happened, though, she made no property settlement with her husband, because on a night a little more than a week later she was killed, and all her property, not just part, became Steven's.

Now, seated at the window in the fading light, Judith remembered the sounds which had awakened her the night of Cecily's death, that August night nearly a year in the past. Heavy footsteps on the outside stairs, and a knock at the door. Confused and alarmed, Judith sat up in bed and called out, "Who's there?"

"Police, miss. Inspector Gregson, C.I.D. Open the door, please. I must talk to you."

She had switched on the bedside lamp and seen that the hands of the small clock on the nightstand pointed to almost two-thirty, Heartbeats rapid, she put on slippers and a navy flannel robe and went to the door. The tall, heavyset plainclothesman who stood on the small landing was about fifty, with a courteous look about him. But he was not too courteous to tell her, within seconds after she let him into the apartment, that her cousin had been murdered. Even as she gasped with shock, Judith was dimly aware of his purpose in being so blunt. He wanted to judge from her reaction whether or not the news came to her as a complete surprise.

She asked dazedly, "How—how was she—"

"Someone used some sort of cutting instrument to sever the spinal cord at the back of her neck. Probably she was asleep at the time. There is no sign that she struggled."

"When—"

"We're not sure, of course, but the medical examiner gives it as a quick judgment that she died sometime between ten-thirty and midnight. Did you hear anything during that time?"

Judith could not shake off a sense—or perhaps it was a hope—that the burly policeman's presence here in this familiar room, and what he had just told her, were nothing but an especially vivid dream.

"No. I was asleep by ten. Just before I went to bed I

looked over at the main house. It seemed perfectly quiet. There weren't even any lights showing at the back of the house, although I suppose there were at the front."

"And you slept undisturbed? You didn't even hear a car driving in, or driving away?"

"No." After a moment she added, "Who was it who called the police?"

"Mr. Grenville. He says he came home about twelve-thirty or a quarter of one and went upstairs. The door to his wife's room was open, and enough light fell into the room from the hall for him to see that there was something wrong. He went into the room, turned on the light, and then called the police."

"Did—did he say where he had been?"

"Yes, in London, at a dinner of the Architectural Society. Why do you ask?"

"I just wondered."

He did not leave it at that, of course. "Didn't Mr. and Mrs. Grenville get on well?"

He could learn the truth from scores of others, so there was no point in lying. "They got along very badly."

He looked at her searchingly for a moment and then got to his feet. "We'll want a formal statement from you tomorrow. Goodnight, Miss Dunne, and thank you."

When he had gone she moved reluctantly to her living room window. The draperies of that corner room were open wide. Men, at least three of them, were moving around in the glare of the ceiling light. As Judith watched, one of them lifted a camera and looked through its viewer. Even though the bed was outside her line of vision, Judith knew that he must be taking pictures of the lifeless girl who lay upon it. Shuddering, she reached up and drew her own window draperies closed. Then, because she knew she would get no more sleep that night, she dressed, went into the kitchen, and brewed coffee.

For two weeks after that police questioned Cecily's friends and the men who had been at that architectural dinner in London. Their efforts did not result in an arrest. Steven Grenville's story held up, and no other suspects were uncovered among Cecily's associates. No trace of a weapon was found. Inspector Gregson, when he returned to get Judith's statement the day after Cecily's death, remarked that in all likelihood the cleaver or whatever the killer had used was now at the bottom of the Thames.

Judith did not spend those two weeks in the carriage-house apartment. The afternoon following the night of Cecily's death she drove into the village and stopped before a semidetached stucco house with a hand-lettered sign in its lace-curtained front window: "Bed-sitting room to let, with kitchen privileges." After paying the householder, a middle-aged widow, ten pounds for the first week's rent, she drove back to the apartment and packed her things. She was moving not so much because of her cousin's death as because of her cousin's husband. Innocent though in all probability he was, she did not relish the thought of spending her nights a stone's throw from the house where Steven Grenville now lived alone.

She had worked feverishly hard during those two weeks last August, not only to distract herself but because she knew she must finish the sketches for Barney's book before she returned to him. When at the end of the two weeks she asked the police for permission to leave England it was granted to her. At Heathrow Airport she requested and received permission to take the precious sketches in their large carrying case into the plane's cabin with her. Seven hours later, when at Kennedy she had gone through customs, she saw Barney waiting for her beyond the barrier. But the look on his face told her that something was wrong, very wrong—

Abruptly she got up from the table beside the window and switched on the lamp. She didn't want to think about that reunion with Barney that had been no reunion at all, nor about the lonely bitter fall and winter months that had followed. Once more she was going to illustrate a Barney Wallace book. And perhaps this time they would regain and keep a private happiness together as well as professional success.

She carried her plate and salad bowl and fork into the kitchen and washed them. After spreading the dish towel to dry, she hesitated for a moment and then drew the step-stool up to the tall cupboard. She climbed the stool and then reached a groping hand to the cupboard's top. Her fingers encountered cool metal. Yes, there it was, her cousin's automatic, the gun Judith had left hidden up there when she fled this apartment last summer for that bed-sitting room in the village.

Now that she was really alone here, with no one at all living in the main house, and no near neighbors, perhaps it was just as well that she had a gun. She descended from the step-stool and then, as Cecily had showed her how to do, took out the automatic's clip. Yes, the gun was still loaded. She carried it into the bedroom and placed it in the drawer of the stand beside her bed. She had just returned to the living room when the phone rang.

"Judith?" a vaguely familiar voice said. "It's Diana Sherill."

"Why, Diana! How nice to hear from you." As she spoke she thought, as she often had last summer, of how misnamed Diana was. Plump and blond and snub-nosed, she in no way resembled a goddess of the chase.

"George told me that you've applied for permission to

36

make more sketches at the palace this summer." George Sherill, Diana's husband, was an employee of Great Britain's Department of the Environment. Each morning he left his ultramodern London flat and drove to his office, located off a vaulted and stone-flagged corridor in the oldest part of the ancient palace.

"Yes, I wrote to him from New York but I didn't have time to wait for a reply. There won't be any trouble about getting permission, will there?"

"Of course not. George has already arranged it. But please don't plunge into work before we have even seen each other. How about lunch on Thursday? Let's go to an Italian place I know in Soho. The food's good, and Soho is always interesting." She giggled. "Raunchy, but interesting."

"Please give me a rain check on it. I'm sorry, but I do want to get some solid work done during the first few days." She really was sorry. She had liked Diana better than any of Cecily's other friends, although come to think of it, the Sherills were more Steven Grenville's friends than Cecily's. It was because both Steven and George were connected with Hampton Court Palace that the two couples had met.

"Judith, please. I do want to see you. Please lunch with me."

Diana's tone, offhand only minutes ago, held urgency now. Judith asked, "What is it? I mean, is there some special reason—"

"Not really." Judith felt sure that the other girl was lying. "But please have lunch with me. Surely you can take a few hours away from your drawing board."

"All right," Judith said reluctantly. "Day after tomorrow. Will one o'clock be all right?"

"One will be fine." Now that she had carried her point, Diana's voice once more was jaunty. "The restaurant is called Rocco's, and it's on Greek Street. I'll meet you there."

When she had hung up Judith stood with her hand on the phone for a moment, wondering what giggly, light-minded Diana Sherill could be worried about. Well, she would find out on Thursday. She glanced at her watch. Five past ten. Best to get to sleep if she could.

But although it was ten o'clock in London it was only five in the afternoon in New York, and her mind and body were still on New York time. Thus, after she went to bed she did not go to sleep. Instead she stared up into the darkness, going over in her mind the sketches she and Barney had agreed upon before she left New York. She intended to depict the Stuart monarchs in order, starting with dour James the First, shooter of tame deer and sponsor of the King James version of the Bible, and ending with Anne, the fat, greedy queen whose name, paradoxically, had been given to one of the most graceful products of the furniture maker's art. And in between she would sketch James's tragic son, five-feet-tall Charles the First, slipping out of a Hampton Court Palace window to begin a flight that ultimately led him, not to safety, but the block. She would sketch Charles the Second, strolling through the palace gardens with his buxom mistresses and his long-eared spaniels, while fifteen miles away in London carts carrying heaped-up victims of the Black Death creaked through the deserted streets—

A wind was rising. Judith could hear it see the through the tall elms that lined one side of the driveway. Now it was at her bedroom window, bellying the curtains inward, stirring the edge of the shade so that it rattled against the raised sash. Best to run the shade higher, so that the wind could not reach it.

She swung out of bed, crossed to the window, and

raised the sash high. Then she stood looking at the dark rear wall of the main house. A three-quarter's moon was up now. She could see its silvery reflection in the glass of that corner window.

Suddenly she stiffened. For just a second or two, warmer light had mingled with the moon's reflection. There it was again, a soft, wavering glow like that of a candle. Now it had disappeared. It was as if the wind had sent a draught wandering through that supposedly empty house over there, parting the draperies at that corner window so that light shone through to mingle with the moon's reflection.

That house was not empty, not at the moment. Someone was over there in the room where Cecily had met her violent death.

4

With the illogical feeling that the prowler over there might look through that slit in the draperies and see her at her own darkened window, she pulled the shade clear to the sill. Then she stood indecisive in the deeper darkness. What should she do? Call the village police? Yes, that would be the sensible thing to do, except that the police, to make sure of catching the intruder, would need to approach the house quietly. And they could not do that unless she slipped out of her apartment before their arrival and unlocked the gate in the brick wall. Her stomach knotted up at the thought of walking down the drive between the house wall and the row of wind-lashed trees to the gate. She pictured herself there, fumbling with the heavy key, while a dark figure emerged from that supposedly deserted house and glided silently toward her through the knee-high grass—

The solution came to her. Call Steven Grenville at his flat in the village. He would phone the police, and then follow them out here, or even ride with them, and open the gate. She moved cautiously through the darkness to the nightstand beside her bed and picked up her luminous-dialed watch. Not quite eleven-thirty. Probably he hadn't even gone to bed yet.

Afraid to turn on lights lest she alert the intruder over there, she groped her way into the living room. She had left the draperies open there, and the shade up, and so the darkness was less complete. She moved down the short hall to the kitchen and, after a certain amount of fumbling, managed to open the middle drawer in the counter that stretched along one wall. If she remembered correctly, last summer there had been a pencil-sized flashlight in that drawer. Her groping fingers, first encountering candle ends and a ball of twine, finally fastened around the flashlight. She carried it back into the living room and, after closing the draperies, turned on the flashlight and laid it on the end table beside the telephone. From the table's shelf she took the phone book and, seated on the sofa, looked up Steven Grenville's number.

She let the phone ring seven times. Eight. Nine. No matter how soundly asleep, he should have awakened by then.

She hung up and looked at the drawn chintz draperies, gleaming faintly in the flashlight's refracted glow. So Steven was not in his flat. Was he, instead, over there in that room where his wife had been murdered? Well, he had every right to be there. It was his house. And yet the thought of him paying a nocturnal visit to that room was singularly unpleasant.

She switched off the flashlight and then crossed through the darkness to the window. She parted the draperies. The moon's reflection had withdrawn from that window over there. Now its pane appeared only as a faintly gleaming black rectangle set in the dark wall. She watched for several minutes, but although she could still feel the wind and hear it seething through the trees, and although eddies of air no doubt still swirled through that house to stir the draperies of that corner room, she saw no wavering yellow glow.

She began to doubt that there ever had been a light in

that room tonight. Window glass, especially in old houses, often had imperfections. And in old houses, too, window panes were often loose in their frames, loose enough to rattle in the wind. Perhaps when gusts intermittently shook that windowpane over there, some flaw in the glass momentarily had reflected the moonlight as a gleam of pale yellow rather than silver.

On the other hand, maybe there had been someone there, someone who in these last few minutes might have descended the stairs of that empty house and then, by one means or another, slipped out into the night. But one thing was certain. Before going to Hampton Court Palace tomorrow, she would tell Steven Grenville about this.

She made certain that her apartment door was still locked. And although she realized that no one could reach her windows except with a ladder, she closed and latched them. But even so, once she had gone to bed, she found she was still too upset to sleep. It was not until she saw the first gray light, and heard the drowsy dawn notes of birds, that she slipped into unconsciousness.

She awoke to a flood of sunlight through the closed window. The hands of her watch pointed to a quarter past ten. She got out of bed and crossed to the window. As she raised the sash and leaned out into the bright morning, her fears of the night before began to seem absurd. The house beyond the overgrown rear lawn looked melancholy, as uninhabited houses often do, but it did not look sinister.

Just the same, as soon as she had finished breakfast, she walked down the driveway to the main house and began to check its locks. The back door was locked, and the wide doorway to the windowless garage was firmly padlocked. She went on down the drive past the north wall of the house, pausing at each long window to test the curving bars of the protective iron grilles. None of them was loose. At the front of the house the thick-paneled white door was locked. She moved on around the corner, testing window grilles as she went, and, after moving along the garage's windowless rear wall, cut across the back lawn to her own staircase. Obviously no one, at least no one who did not have a key, had been in that house last night. She was glad that she had not called the police. Perhaps it would be best not to say anything to Steven Grenville, either.

But ten minutes later, as she started down the driveway in the Volvo, she braked to a stop. A wisteria vine, probably planted many decades ago at the northeast corner of the house, now reached clear to the roof. It also had spread toward the north window of that corner bedroom, a window at right angles to the one through which, the night before, she had thought she had seen a wavering light. She looked at the vine for several seconds. Then she drove down to the gate, unlocked it and, after relocking it behind her, drove to the village.

That dark green Mercedes Cecily had insisted upon driving from Heathrow Airport that May morning more than a year ago was parked in front of Steven's office. Judith went inside. Miss Claverly was not seated behind her desk. After a moment's hesitation, Judith walked to the door of the inner office and knocked. Steven called, in an absent-minded tone, "Come in."

She opened the door. Bent over the drafting table he said, eyes still fixed on outspread blueprints, "Just put the coffee down anywhere."

When she neither moved nor spoke, he looked up. The surprise in his eyes gave way to displeasure. "Sorry. I thought you were Miss Claverly. I sent her out for coffee." He paused. "What can I do for you?"

His tone made it clear that what she could do for him

43

was to leave as soon as possible. Her own hostility rose, and her distrust with it. She said, "I think that there was a prowler in your house around eleven o'clock last night."

"My house?"

"The Columns. I understood that you still own it. I checked all the doors and window grilles this morning and they seemed all right, but just the same—"

"If you saw no evidence of a break-in, there was no prowler. Except for myself, the estate agent with whom I listed the house is the only person with a key. And he would not be showing a prospective tenant through the house at that time of night. What makes you think there was a prowler?"

"I thought I saw a light in—" She stopped. No matter how she felt about him, she could not bring herself to say, "the room in which your wife was murdered." And so she said, "I thought I saw a light in the northeast corner room, upstairs."

"You could not have seen a light in any room. The electricity is off."

"It could have been a flashlight! Or more likely a candle. I mean, the light seemed to waver. But it was hard to be sure of anything. The window pane was reflecting the moonlight."

"Are you sure you saw anything besides moonlight?"

She had expected him to ask that. "No, I'm not sure. But since it is your house, I should think you would want to investigate. In fact, I called you last night, with the thought that you might want to tell the police, but there was no answer."

"Of course not. I was out."

Plainly he did not intend to tell her where he had been. She wanted to ask, "Were you in that corner room last night?" But such a question would be not only rude but futile. If he had been there, he would not admit it.

He said, "Perhaps you have a theory as to how a prowler without a key can get into a securely locked house without breaking locks or removing window grilles."

"As a matter of fact I do. Upstairs windows are often left unlocked. And there's a wisteria vine growing past the north window of that corner room clear to the roof."

From the startled look in his eyes she saw that he realized she might be right. After a moment he said, "Very well. I'll see if there are any signs that anyone beside the estate agent and prospective tenants have been in that house. I can't imagine why anyone else would want to go in there. There's nothing worth stealing. Cecily's furs and jewelry were sold six months ago to help pay the inheritance taxes. As for the furniture, I put the few good pieces in storage."

He did not need to tell Judith that the "few good pieces" had been Grenville heirlooms, inherited from his grandmother soon after he and Cecily had married. The rest of the furniture was nineteen-twentyish stuff which had been in the house when Cecily's father bought it for her, plus a few items Cecily herself had added—a bar and barstools upholstered in silver vinyl in what once had been the library, and, in the large living room, flashing strobe lights that could be turned on to accompany rock music, whether live or on tape.

He went on, "Perhaps you'd like to accompany me when I look through the house. That way you could satisfy yourself that there's no evidence of anyone breaking in. Of course, perhaps you've decided now that you do not want to stay in the apartment."

Obviously he hoped that was the case. But she had no intention of leaving that apartment. She had to get those illustrations done. It was important not only for her bank account and her career, but for her future relationship with Barney. And she could not afford, while she did her work, to live in rented quarters.

She said coolly, "No, I intend to stay where I am."

After a moment he answered, "Very well. Could you be back at The Columns by four this afternoon?"

"I could."

"I will meet you there."

She nodded. "Goodbye," she said, and walked through the outer office to the street. Miss Claverly was coming along the sidewalk, a paper bag in her hand. Judith waited, smiling, until the older woman reached her, and then said, "I want to thank you for making up the bed in my apartment, and putting towels in the bathroom. It was a pleasant surprise."

"It was no trouble, Miss Dunne. And I know how it is when you've traveled a long way to get someplace, and then find you have to do a lot of little things before you can rest. Well, I'd better take Mr. Grenville his coffee before it gets cold. He says he'll need it to get him through the morning. I guess he didn't sleep very well last night."

"Thanks again," Judith said, "And goodbye for now."

She got into the rented car, drove across the cement bridge spanning the Thames, and stopped at the wide gateway to the palace. The uniformed guard on duty moved toward her smiling. "Good morning, miss." He had forgotten her name, or perhaps never known it, but obviously he remembered her face. "Back with us to draw more pictures this summer?"

"Yes. At least I hope I am. I haven't received my formal permission from Mr. Sherill yet. Do you think it will be all right for me to leave my car in the administration car park?"

"I don't see why not, miss. You did last year."

46

She drove on. Ahead rose the palace's mighty west front of red brick, with its huge oriel window of white stone above the arched entrance, and its turrets and mullioned windows and crenelated battlements stretching to either side. As always, the façade of this great structure built by the butcher's son delighted her eyes. And, as often happened, she felt a pang of sympathy for poor Wolsey, whose sovereign had rewarded him for years of loyal and expert service by seizing his palace and sentencing him to death. Judith knew it was absurd to dislike a man who had died four hundred years ago, and yet she could not think of Henry the Eighth without feeling distaste.

Just before reaching the bridge that led over a moat to the palace entrance, she turned left and parked her car behind a long, low structure of red brick, built in the eighteenth century as a troop barracks, but now given over to machine and carpentry shops. From there she walked along the northern side of the palace and then turned through an archway. Beyond was a corridor paved with stones worn hollow by centuries of footsteps. To her left was a partially opened door of heavy oak. She pushed it farther open and stepped over the threshhold.

It was like stepping from the early sixteenth century into the late twentieth. Fluorescent light shone down on steel filing cabinets, and on an electric typewriter and the girl using it. Last summer George Sherill's secretary had been a petite redhead with dimples. This one was a brunette with a short, swingy haircut of the sort popularized by a skating star, and cool gray eyes accented with green eye shadow.

She said, "May I help you?"

"My name is Judith Dunne. I think Mr. Sherill is expecting me."

The girl behind the desk flipped a lever on the intercom. George Sherill's voice, sounding tinny, said, "Yes?"

"Miss Judith Dunne is here to see you."

There was a moment's silence. Then: "Send her in, please."

When Judith entered the inner office George Sherill was already on his feet, lips smiling and one well-cared-for hand extended. George was a well-cared-for-looking man, only of medium height, but with a flat-waisted figure that made the most of his inches, and brown eyes set in a face he kept tanned by use of a sunlamp. Only his straight brown hair, receding from his temples, hinted that he was forty.

"Judith! How nice to see you. Sit down, sit down." Then, when they were both seated: "As soon as I received your letter I applied for your authorization." He reached into a desk drawer and handed her a long envelope. "Here it is, in writing. Sketch away as much as you please."

"Thank you." She put the envelope into her shoulder bag.

"Diana tells me you two girls are lunching together tomorrow."

"That's right."

"Good. And I hope you will have dinner with both of us before long. Now this new book you will illustrate. Is it by the same author?"

"Yes, but this one deals with the Stuart monarchs who lived here. Today I'm going over to Bushey Park and draw James the First taking pot shots at tame deer."

"Good lord, did he do that? I know that he filled the palace with his boy friends, but I didn't know about the deer."

"Cecily told me that story last summer. I looked it up and found it was true."

"I see."

48

She waited for him to go on, but he let the silence lengthen awkwardly. She got to her feet and so did he. "Well, thanks very much, George. I had better get to work now."

When she had gone George Sherill stared down at his desk. He hated the thought of Judith spending the summer here, and even more the thought of her and his wife getting together. For months now Diana had been behaving strangely, bringing the conversation again and again to Cecily Grenville, almost as if she suspected—well, at least something.

Probably over lunch tomorrow Diana would bring up the subject of the dead girl, hoping Judith Dunne could furnish additional information about her. And perhaps she could. After all, even though the American girl and Cecily had not had much in common, they were cousins, and they had lived last summer within a stone's throw of one another. Perhaps Judith knew things about her cousin she had not told the police. There could even be things she had forgotten she knew, but would remember under Diana's probing.

Why had he ever gotten mixed up with Cecily Grenville, a dangerous girl who practically went around asking to get herself killed? Why was he such a fool where women were concerned? Well, Diana was part of the reason. He should never have married her, a not-very-bright girl whose prettiness, insipid even when it had been at its best, was now obscured by overweight. But she had believed herself to be pregnant, and he had feared that if she or her family made a fuss he might lose his position—

Later they learned that she could not have children. If she had been able to, perhaps their marriage would not have been so galling for him. At least then she would have been too busy to spend all her time watching him, suspecting him, questioning him. With a wife like that almost any man might be driven to making a fool of himself.

The Cecily Grenville case had not been closed. No murder case ever was. If the police learned enough to start questioning him again—Well, at the very least Her Majesty's Government would give him the sack, and at the very worst—

God, he felt awful. Sometimes he wondered if nerve strain had not affected his mind.

He stared at the closed door to the outer office. When he had hired his new secretary two weeks ago he had told himself that it was because she was an excellent typist and had a pleasant telephone voice. This time, he had promised himself, there would be no hanky-panky.

But he desperately needed distraction. Distraction from worry, from memory. He needed it especially now that the Dunne girl had come back, increasing his burden of anxiety.

He sat motionless for a moment and then flipped the intercom. "Helen, will you come in here, please?"

She opened the door, shorthand notebook in her left hand. When she had closed the door behind her he said, "Why don't you go home?" Home to her was a flat in the town of Richmond, four miles away. "I mean, take the afternoon off."

She looked at him questioningly. "I have an errand over in Richmond this afternoon," he went on. "You might ask me to drop in for a drink—oh, around three o'clock."

She smiled. "Why don't you drop in for a drink around three o'clock?"

5

JUDITH RETRACED her steps to the car park and took her drawing case out of the Volvo's boot. Then she walked north, passing the outdoor restaurant where, on this weekday morning, only a few people sat at the round tables, and past the famous maze, that labyrinth of six-feet-high yew and privet hedges set out three hundred years ago. In those days the maze had been a pleasant, easily solved puzzle for courtiers and their ladies, and a place for amorous dalliance. Now it was chiefly the very young who delighted in trying to find their way through the labyrinth. Although they were invisible behind the hedges, Judith could hear the high, excited voices of several children.

She crossed a road into the thousand-plus acres of long, tangled grass, of giant oaks and beeches and elms, of meandering streams and lily-choked ponds known as Bushey Park. The giant rhododendrons were still in bloom. A solid wall of them lined the winding path along which she moved. She crossed a footbridge, circled around a clump of bushes, and found herself in a remembered spot, a little glade filled with tall bracken. On the far side of the glade a circular wooden bench had been built around the trunk of an oak tree. She was not surprised to see a fallow deer lying in the ferns, head raised, round eyes regarding her with mild interest. More often than not when she visited this glade the previous summer there had been a deer taking his ease here. Perhaps it was always the same animal.

She carried her sketching case over to the oak and took out her folding easel. When she had the easel set up and her drawing paper thumbtacked into place, she began to sketch the semicircle of trees and bracken and the resting deer. Soon she was so absorbed in her work that she was only dimly aware of the constant hum of bees hovering over a nearby cluster of yellow-flowered ligularia, and of the voices of occasional groups of people moving along the path several yards away.

When she had finished the background she took a small picture from the flat case, a photograph of a painting of James the First, and thumbtacked it to the left-hand corner of the easel. Then she sketched His Majesty peering, musket in hand, from behind a tree. She drew him wearing, not the white ruff and embroidered waistcoat and short, puffed breeches of his portrait, but a hunting costume of his own devising which had been much laughed at by his guests at Hampton Court. With a jauntily peaked and feathered cap topping his dour Scots visage, and a hunting horn dangling at his side in place of a sword, he looked like an aging and ill-tempered Robin Hood.

When she had finished the sketch she sat back and studied it. She felt a twinge of guilt, almost as if King James's ghost might be looking indignantly over her shoulder. Well, she would balance this sketch with one of him presiding at a Hampton Court meeting of Anglican and Puritan clergymen, where he had disputed with the bishops "wisely, wittily, and learnedly," and had decreed that a new translation of the Bible be made.

One thing she was certain of. When she showed her

drawings to Barney a couple of months from now, he would like especially the one she had done today.

As sometimes happened, she was stabbed with the painful memory of the last time she had carried a caseful of drawings back across the Atlantic to Barney. She thought of the bewilderment she had felt when, in the long room beyond the customs counters, he had given her a strained little smile and then kissed her, not on the lips but the cheek. Asking strangely impersonal questions—was the flight smooth and how was the food and had she watched the movie?—he escorted her across the road to the parking lot.

They got into his car. As he started the engine Judith asked, puzzled and chilled, "Is there anything wrong?"

He was silent for a moment and then said rapidly, "Well, yes. There is—a problem. But let's not discuss it until after we've gone to your place and looked at the drawings. Okay?"

Torn, filled with anxiety, and yet just as glad to postpone learning what caused his strangeness, she said, "Okay."

In her walkup apartment on East Twenty-third Street she had placed the pile of drawings on the floor. She and Barney had sat on the rug, inspecting her sketches of the earliest rulers who had lived at Hampton Court Palace —fat and cruel King Henry and his various wives, the invalid boy king Edward the Sixth and his almost equally unhealthy half-sister, fated to go down in history as Bloody Mary, and, finally, resplendent Elizabeth the First.

At last Barney said, "They're good, Judy, awfully good. I'm glad, not just for my sake but for yours. You'll get plenty of assignments after this. At the same time, the wonderful job you've done makes it all the harder to tell you—what I have to tell you."

He fell silent. Judith cried, "For God's sake, don't be a sadist. Tell me!"

"All right. I've fallen in love with someone else. I'm in love with my agent."

She felt a rising hysteria. "Have you gone crazy? Your agent is around fifty-five, married, and a grandfather."

"I guess I didn't mention it in any of my letters, but I got a new agent six weeks ago. Her name is Thea Froissart."

Judith knew the name. Some of Thea Froissart's clients were best-selling writers. Some were darlings of the critics. A few were both.

"I met her at a party—"

"Sure," Judith said in a thickened voice. "Just the way you met me."

He reddened, but went on doggedly, "She said she'd happened to see a book of mine her nephew had gotten as a birthday present. She said she'd enjoyed it, but she felt that she could help me to write far more important books. One thing led to another and—well, now we're in love. I'm sorry, Judith, but when these things happen, they happen."

She said nothing, merely looked at him with brown eyes whose pupils had expanded so that they looked black in her white face.

"She's—she's jealous of you, Judy. She doesn't want us to work together again. I suppose that's only natural."

Still Judith said nothing.

"Shall I take the sketches to Coram and Daniels, Judy?" Coram and Daniels were his publishers. "I'm sure they'll be awfully pleased with them."

"Yes, take them." Still seated on the floor, she watched him gather up the drawings she had made with double delight, not just the joy of creation, but the pleasure of knowing they would enhance a book written by a man she hoped to spend the rest of her life with.

At the door he turned back to her. "Judy, I hated to tell you this, hated it like the very devil. But I hope you'll look at it this way. One very good thing came out of your getting mixed up with me. It expanded your talent. These drawings are the best you've ever done."

"And I owe it all to you! Gee! Thanks a heap, Barney."

His flush deepened. "Goodbye, Judy." He went out.

In the weeks that followed she was glad that she had protected her pride, glad that she hadn't wept or pleaded. But pride was a cold substitute for a lover. And it did nothing to lessen the devastating effect unhappiness had upon her work. Pleased with her Hampton Court drawings, Coram and Daniels twice had asked her to submit sample illustrations for a book by another of the firm's authors. Neither time had she been able to turn out acceptable work. Fortunately, Coram and Daniels had paid her well for illustrating Barney's book. Fortunately, too, she had a fairly large savings account. Just the same, by mid-May she had decided that she must either find a job with some commercial art firm or go back to Kentucky. Then one night Barney had phoned.

"Look, I wouldn't blame you for hanging up on me, but please don't. I want to see you, Judith."

"Why?" She hated it that, after the months of unhappiness he had cost her, the sound of his voice could make her pulses race, not with anger, but longing.

"Let's say it's business. I'm halfway through the final draft of a new book on Hampton Court, and I'd like you to illustrate it for me."

"Won't Thea Froissart object?"

"That's been over for weeks."

"You mean she's no longer your agent?"

"We're no longer anything to each other. At the moment, I don't have an agent. Now will you have dinner with me tomorrow night? Please, Judy!"

She did. And after one more date with him she agreed to illustrate his new book. But despite his obvious regret that he had ever turned away from her, and his obvious hope that they would resume their affair, she had managed to keep their relationship strictly professional.

But when she went back to New York weeks from now? Unseeingly she stared at the dappled light-and-shadow the wind-stirred branches of the oak tree cast over the long grass. When she went back to New York, she felt sure, she would no longer fight against the attraction he held for her. True, perhaps she never again would trust him completely. But it seemed to her that possible mistrust was outweighed by other factors—his undiminished physical appeal for her, and the success with which they had collaborated, and his obvious regret for having turned away from her.

She looked at her watch. Two-thirty. No wonder she was hungry. She would have lunch at that outdoor self-service restaurant and then keep her appointment with Steven Grenville at The Columns.

In the restaurant she discovered that since last summer there had been no improvement in the British-style ham sandwich. It still consisted of a razor-thin slice of ham—almost too thin to be detected by taste—between two thick slices of bread. Both annoyed and amused, she reflected that the English, having invented the sandwich two centuries ago, by now should have learned how to make one. But the understuffed English sandwich, like the unworkable public telephone, was one of the few things she had found to deplore on this green and pleasant island.

When she had finished her sandwich and her tea, she went back to the Volvo and placed the sketching case in the boot. Then on impulse she walked a few yards, turned onto the moat bridge with its facing rows of gargoyle-like stone beasts—grimacing monkeys and snarling lions and leering goats—and then walked under an archway into Base Court, the first and largest of the palace's several courtyards. She lingered there for several minutes, looking up at the mullioned windows on the northern side of the court. Judith knew that for at least two hundred years the rooms behind those windows had housed visitors who came to Hampton Court to be lavishly entertained with tournaments, stag hunts, and banquets that lasted six hours. Now that part of the palace, as well as others, was given over to apartments where, by grace-and-favor of Her Majesty Elizabeth the Second, widowed ladies watched television, and entertained each other at tea.

Her gaze moved to the northeastern corner of the court and the looming roof of Henry the Eighth's Great Hall, where in all probability Shakespeare had acted in plays, including some of his own, during Christmas seasons. From there her eyes roamed over the eastern side of the court to an archway which led to the next courtyard and which was called Anne Boleyn's gateway, because King Henry had embellished its ceiling with her initials and his own during her brief months as his queen.

A glance at her watch told Judith that she had no more time today to renew her acquaintance with Hampton Court. Already it was almost four. She had nearly reached the entrance when she heard rapid footsteps behind her over the centuries-old brick paving. She turned. Kyle Hodge moved toward her, smiling. "I saw you from up there," he said, and gestured toward a window in the court's northern wall. "I thought I'd come down to see how your work is going."

She returned his smile. "All right, I think. I did James the First over in Bushey Park today."

"Sneaking shots at tame deer?"

"So you know about that."

"I should. After all, I teach history." He paused. "May I ask you to join my mother and me for a cup of tea?"

She said sincerely, "I wish I could, but I have a four o'clock appointment."

"Well, perhaps some other time."

"Of course. I'll be here all summer. Goodbye," she said, and turned away.

Standing tall and gaunt at the window of her apartment, Flora Hodge looked down at her son. He still stood there, gazing after that American girl as she moved toward the archway. Obviously she had not accepted Kyle's tea invitation, which from Mrs. Hodge's point of view was good. Obviously, too, he was very disappointed, and that was bad.

Not that Flora Hodge had anything against the girl. She had seemed nice enough on the few occasions last summer when Mrs. Hodge had exchanged a few words with her. But after all she was a cousin of that rich trollop, Cecily Grenville. Judith had lived on Cecily's property last summer, and no doubt gone to Cecily's parties, and people knew what had gone on *there*. Drinking and drug-taking and others things a decent person didn't even want to think about. No, Judith Dunne could not be as nice as she seemed.

And so Kyle must not become interested in her, he must not! There must not be a repetition of what she, his mother, had gone through the previous summer. Flora recalled the first time she became aware that her son was drawn to the Grenville woman. She and Kyle had been returning home after an afternoon's stroll by the river. As they approached the palace's western entrance,

Cecily and that architect husband of hers had emerged from Base Court and started across the moat bridge. For some reason Flora glanced at her son, and saw him looking at the girl with naked longing in his eyes.

Fear had squeezed Flora's heart. Because Steven Grenville had to approve the plans for all repair work at Hampton Court, he frequently was at the palace. Fairly frequently, too, his wife came here. How long before she became aware of Kyle's handsome face and that look in his eyes?

Well, the Grenville woman was dead now, Flora thought grimly, and no longer a worry. But she still wondered how it was that her son, with his leftist notions, could have fancied a rich, idle, useless girl like Cecily, no matter how good looking. Not that Flora shared her son's notions. A firm believer in the class system, she had voted conservative all her life. *She* didn't mind that the other grace-and-favor tenants did not include her in their dinner parties and London theater parties. Kyle resented that, but she did not. It was enough that she could live in this nice apartment. It was enough that she and Lady Marsden and Lady Dawling and the others exchanged polite greetings when they met in the corridors or on the palace grounds. Outside of that —well, people should stick to their own kind.

She reflected that it was her own sister, Kyle's Aunt Sara, who had influenced him to think as he did. After the death of Kyle's father, a clerk in a tobacconist's shop, it had been necessary for Flora to go back to work as a nursemaid. Few families would allow her to keep her small son with her, and so he had spent a lot of his time, from early childhood clear through his university years, with Sara. She was the one who had told him that old story—a story that might not even be true—about how an ancestor of theirs had gotten what the Americans call a raw deal. Maybe that had given him ideas about injustice in general, until finally he'd decided that the whole world ought to be changed around. And that was silly. Bright, hard-working people always could get on. Look at Kyle himself, for instance, a history master now, and probably someday a headmaster. Why did he have to worry over that social injustice he was always talking about?

He had turned around now and was moving toward the entrance, invisible to her, to the stairs which led to this apartment. For another second or two she looked at the top of his dark head, feeling a possessive love for her intelligent and handsome son, and an impatience with those "notions" of his, and a fierce determination that only a girl worthy of him would ever get him.

If anyone had told her that she would never consider any girl worthy of him, she would have denied it vigorously.

She hurried across the parlor and into the kitchen. Now that the Dunne girl wasn't coming up here for tea, she would serve Kyle's favorite jam, wild strawberry, along with the scones.

6

As JUDITH NEARED The Columns she saw Steven Grenville's Mercedes parked at the roadside just beyond the gate in the high brick wall. The gate stood open. She drove down the drive and stopped beside the flagstone walk which ran along the front of the house. Farther down the drive, below the northern window of that corner room, stood a light truck. Between the truck and the wall a man in blue coveralls knelt on the narrow grassy strip, sawing away at the roots of that giant wisteria vine. Standing beside him, Steven said something to the man, and then walked to Judith's car and opened its door.

"I've asked Clancy over there to start taking down that wisteria," Steven said, as she stepped out of the car. "Tomorrow he'll be back with a ladder and tear the upper part of it loose."

"It seems a pity, a beautiful old vine like that."

A lift of his eyebrow reminded her that she was the one who had suggested that a prowler could climb that vine to an upstairs window. But all he said was, "I haven't looked inside the house yet. Shall we go in?"

As she looked at his bony, unsmiling face she felt a sudden uneasiness about going into that empty house with him, even in broad daylight. Then she realized how absurd she was. She would be in no danger, not when the coveralled man could testify that she and Steven had entered the house together. She said, "All right."

Steven unlocked the front door and then left her standing in the dim lower hall while he went through an archway into the living room. She heard drapery rings sliding on their rods. Light fell through the archway onto the foot of brown-carpeted stairs.

When he returned to her Steven said, "There's a woman who comes in twice a month to dust the place. She said it was best to keep the draperies drawn, so that the rugs and furniture won't fade. I told her to do as she liked."

They climbed the stairs and turned left along a brown-carpeted hall illuminated by an uncurtained window at its end. Beside the closed door of that rear corner room he hesitated. "Better wait here," he said. He went inside, leaving the door slightly ajar.

Again she heard the rattle of drapery rings. "All right," he called.

She stepped into the big room, flooded with light now from both the window facing the carriage-house apartment and the one overlooking the driveway. She had been in this room only twice last summer—both times because Cecily wanted another opinion about some clothes she'd just bought—but Judith remembered it well. The white-brick fireplace which, back in the days before open fires were outlawed in the London area, must have made this large room a cosier place. The wall-to-wall white carpeting. The dressing table of blond wood and the matching chest of drawers. The green brocade chaise longue. The bed canopied in that same brocade. All the furniture was still here except the bed. Judith realized with an inward shrinking why Cecily's husband had gotten rid of that. Any prospective tenant of this house would learn, sooner or later, what had happened here. And he would not relish using a bed upon which a murdered woman had lain.

Now she noticed that even though the bed was missing, something had been added. Two colorfully striped rectangular rugs, probably of Scandinavian origin, lay on the carpet near where the bed had stood. Did they cover bloodstains, or at least discolored patches where bloodstains had been removed? She recalled a police statement that almost surely the clothing of Cecily's killer had been bloodstained. How was it then, Judith wondered for perhaps the twentieth time—that he, or she, had escaped detection?

Steven had moved to the window overlooking the drive. Apparently, just as she had guessed, it was not locked. He slid the sash up, leaned outward for a moment, and then closed the window. "Too bad that the woman who cleans the place was here only two days ago," he said. "If there was dust on the sill we might be able to tell whether or not it had been disturbed by someone coming in through the window."

He moved to the fireplace and ran his hand over the marble mantel. She asked, "What are you doing?"

"Looking for candle grease. You did say the light wavered like a candle flame, didn't you?"

He moved to the chest of drawers and then the dressing table, running his palm over the polished surfaces. Was he, Judith wondered, making fun of her? Or was he giving her story more credence than he had seemed to?

She said, "If the candle was in a saucer or other wide holder, it would not have dripped on the furniture. And if he left the candle here, it may be on the closet shelf."

She crossed the room and slid back the mirrored door of the built-in closet. In the current of disturbed air garments swung on their hangers—long dresses, short dresses, coats, capes, dressing gowns. Shocked, Judith stood motionless for a moment and then turned on him.

"You've just left her clothing hanging here!" When he raised an inquiring eyebrow she went on indignantly, "Don't you know you're not supposed to do that?"

"Why not? The tenants, when I get some, can do what they like with her things."

"But *you* were supposed to do it. You, or somebody who cared for her. When a person dies—"

She broke off, realizing that by the time of her death it was unlikely that anyone really cared for Cecily Grenville. Her parents were dead, her husband alienated, and her friends—real friends, not hangers-on—apparently had been nonexistent.

She said, "When a person dies, the person closest to her is supposed to see that her personal belongings are —are disposed of decently."

His voice was even. "Surely you realized that I was in no way close to Cecily."

Judith blurted out, "Why did you ever marry her?"

When he finally answered his voice was quiet and tired. "Because I loved her. I loved her terribly for more than a year, even though before the first six months were over she had started playing around quite openly. And then suddenly I'd had enough. I no longer loved her."

"Then why didn't you two get a divorce?" As she spoke she was remembering the first time she had asked her cousin that question, one night in this room. Cee-cee had shrugged and answered, "Why should I? At the moment there's no one else I want to marry."

Now Steven said, "I was waiting for her to apply for a divorce. According to the rules I grew up with, a man's supposed to let his wife do that. For me to be the one to sue—well, it would have been the crowning ugliness of something that had started out so beautifully. At least I thought it had."

There was a bitterness in his voice that rang true. No

matter how he had come to feel about Cecily, and no matter what he had done to her, he had loved her once. Judith felt a pang, and after a moment recognized it as a kind of envy. How wonderful it might be to be loved —not temperately, the way Barney loved, never quite losing his cool—but with a fervor which, if too often trampled upon, could turn to the cold disgust she had seen in Steven's face when Cee-cee's behavior was at its most outrageous.

He said, "About her clothes. What do you think should be done?"

After a moment she answered, "I think they should be packed neatly and given to the parish church for their next fund-raising sale."

"Will you do it? I'm sure there are cartons in the attic. I could bring them down here."

"Yes, I'll do it."

"How long will it take you?"

She turned and looked at the long row of garments, and the shoes on their wooden racks on the floor, and the many hat boxes, perhaps containing other things besides hats, on the shelf above. Probably, too, the bureau drawers were filled, and the drawers of the dressing table. She said, facing him, "It will take hours. I'll never be able to finish before dark."

He hesitated. "Very well. I'll leave the key to the front door with you. Then you can come back in tomorrow, and the next day too if you have to."

He turned and left the room. A few moments later she heard footsteps overhead. Soon after that she heard the sound of a car starting up and then moving away down the drive. Evidently the coveralled man, Clancy, had finished severing the vine's roots.

When Steven Grenville came back into the room he was carrying a big paper carton about four feet high. He said, setting it on the rug, "I put half a dozen smaller boxes inside. If those aren't enough, there are more up in the attic. The attic stairs are at the other end of the hall."

"Thank you, but I think these will be enough."

He looked at her for a long moment and then said, "Do you really think you should stay here?"

All her animus toward him came flooding back. "In the carriage-house apartment? Why shouldn't I?"

"Well, if there has been someone prowling around in this house—"

"In this house, not the apartment! Besides, you think I didn't see anything but reflected moonlight."

"I think that is most likely the case. But still, why take a chance? I wouldn't like to see anything happen to you."

I wouldn't like to see anything happen to you. That sentence might have been an expression of slight but honest concern. Or it might have been the expression of a lingering hope that he could rid himself of the presence of a girl who looked like his dead wife. It could even be, she realized, gaze fixed on his unsmiling face, a kind of threat.

"Nothing will happen to me. There's a thumb latch as well as a Yale lock on the apartment door. And there are no wisteria vines leading up to the windows." She paused. "Besides, I have a gun."

He frowned. "You mean you managed to bring a gun with you on your flight from New York?"

"No, Cecily gave it to me, the morning after you blacked her eye. She was afraid that if she kept it she might—use it." She paused. "You did black her eye, didn't you?"

He stared back at her, stony-faced, and then said, "I did. We were quarreling—it doesn't matter now about what—and she came at me with a pair of scissors in her upraised hand. I struck her hand aside and somehow my swing carried through and the edge of my own hand caught her across the eye. I had no idea I'd hit her that hard, because I left the house then. It wasn't until I came back the next evening that I realized how badly bruised she was."

He paused, and then said harshly, "But that's all over. Why question me about it, why wonder about it?"

She thought, maybe I wouldn't wonder, maybe no one would, if we knew who killed your wife. But she said nothing.

Reaching into his pocket he pulled out a key and laid it on the mantelpiece. "That opens the front door. Return it to me when you've finished getting rid of her things."

He left the room. She heard him go down the stairs and out the front door. After an interval she heard the more distant sound of the Mercedes starting up outside the gate.

She drew the dressing table bench across the rug to the closet, climbed up on it, and thoroughly searched the closet shelf. There was no candle up there among the hat boxes, nor did her exploring fingers find the waxiness of congealed candle grease. She descended from the bench and began to pack Cecily's belongings, giving first attention to the contents of the bureau drawers. In one of the smaller cartons she placed sweaters and blouses and scarves, in another underwear and nightgowns. The contents of the dressing table drawers—perfume vials and jars and bottles and small cases holding various cosmetics—filled another box, and shoes from the racks on the closet floor two others. Finally she started taking down garments—day dresses and evening dresses and evening wraps and lounging robes and raincoats—from their padded hangers. Before folding each garment and

67

placing it in the large carton, she went through the pockets to make sure they were empty.

She had thrust her hands into the pockets of a tentlike green polyester housecoat, found them empty, and begun to fold the garment when she heard the crackle of paper. Again she thrust her hand into one of the pockets and discovered what she had missed the first time, a torn seam. She pushed her hand through the opening and down inside the housecoat's lining until her fingers encountered what felt like an envelope.

When she drew it out she saw that it was indeed an envelope, addressed to Cecily, mailed from London, and postmarked August fifth of the previous year. It bore no return address. With a sense of chill Judith realized that her cousin must have received this letter only a day or so before her death. She hesitated momentarily and then took out the single sheet of paper inside the envelope and unfolded it. A typed letter, with neither salutation nor signature, it read:

I must warn you that I cannot go on like this. Call me neurotic, square, overpossessive, or whatever you like, I cannot go on sharing you with others. When I think of you in bed with that soccer player who used to be a Birmingham lorry driver, or that Italian photographer who also likes boys—well, I have a very graphic imagination, and I can no longer bear what goes on in my mind, not and remain sane. Please don't drive me to desperation. Please don't.

Judith could imagine Cecily accepting this letter from the maid, or perhaps picking it up from the hallway carpet below the slot in the front door. After reading it she must have shrugged. Judith could almost see that shrug. Perhaps if there had been a wastebasket handy

Cecily would have dropped the letter, torn to bits, into it. But apparently there had been no wastebasket nearby. And so she had slipped the envelope into the pocket with the torn seam, perhaps intending to destroy the letter sometime later.

Who had written it? Steven? It seemed unlikely that he would write to Cecily when they were living under the same roof. And anyway by last summer, according to him, he had ceased to care what his wife did. But perhaps that indifference was at least partly feigned. Perhaps sometimes—when he was sufficiently drunk, say—he felt a return of his need for her. And as for their living in the same house, Judith knew that a few times last summer Steven had been away. According to Cecily he had been staying at Finchley's, a London club popular with younger architects. Judith thought of him, more than half drunk, typing this letter at a machine in one of the club's public rooms and then going out into the London night to post it.

But certainly it need not have been Steven who wrote it. It could have been any of a number of men. Judith knew only two things for sure about the writer of the letter. He was far from an expert typist. That paragraph contained far more strike-overs and x'd-out mistakes than a person accustomed to typing would have made, however far from sober. The second thing she knew about him was that he had been desperate with jealous pain and rage. With his letter in her hand she could almost feel his desperation throbbing in this silent room —his desperation, and his fear of what it might lead him to do.

She became aware that the light coming through the windows had changed. It was presunset light, faintly reddish. In another half hour the room would begin to fill with shadows. Suddenly she felt a need to be in her own cheerful apartment. She could finish the packing the next afternoon.

She refolded the letter and placed it in its envelope. Later she would decide what, if anything, to do with it. Right now she felt that the one thing she must not do was to place it back inside the lining of that housecoat for some stranger to find. She picked up her shoulder bag from the chaise longue and put the letter inside the zippered side pocket.

After picking up the key Steven had left on the mantelpiece she hurried down the corridor to the head of the stairs. Evidently Steven had redrawn the draperies before he left, because the stairwell and lower hall, illuminated only by faint light from the corridor above, were murky indeed. She knew that she should descend the stairs slowly lest she stumble in the near darkness, but an anxiety had seized her. Clinging to the rail, she hurried down the stairs and then along the hall to the front door. Once she was outside her heartbeats slowed. She locked the door and then looked out across the overgrown lawn to the gate. Had Steven locked it before he left? Probably. Just the same, it would be best to make sure.

He had locked it. She turned and walked back along the drive to her car. As she drove it past the north wall of the house she saw that Clancy had not only severed the vine from its roots but had cut it away from the wall to a height of about eight feet and chopped it into fragments, now lying in a pile at one side of the drive.

She drove her car back to the foot of the apartment steps. As she got out of the car and looked up at the rear window of that corner room she realized for the first time that in her haste to leave she had left the draperies open. Perhaps that was just as well. If a light of any sort appeared in that room tonight, the chances were excellent that she would see it before the intruder realized that the draperies were open.

Not that she expected to see a light. Even if the lower part of the wisteria vine had not been removed, she still would not have expected to see that wavering light, because she had become convinced that either her eyesight or her imagination had been playing tricks the night before. But if an intruder had been up there last night? As she climbed the outside staircase she realized that in her shoulder bag she carried a possible reason for someone's invasion of that room. Perhaps ever since last summer someone had feared that his threatening letter might fall into the hands of the police. Perhaps he had come to that empty house to search for it, not just last night but on former occasions too.

Judith knew that was most unlikely. More than ten months had passed since Cecily's death. Surely by now whoever had written that letter had concluded that either Cecily had destroyed it, or, if it had fallen into the hands of the police, they had given up trying to trace it.

Still, whether or not he had been in that corner room last night, Judith felt sure that the sender of that letter must feel a certain coldness in the pit of his stomach whenever he recalled what he had written.

7

ALTHOUGH AGAIN she was wakeful until well past midnight, once Judith did fall asleep her rest was undisturbed. When she awoke a little before nine she saw that the window draperies of that corner room were still drawn back, just as she had left them. She had a leisurely breakfast, and then called the rectory of the local church. The minister's wife gave her the phone number of a Mrs. Dalrymple, president of the Missionary Society. She would be pleased indeed, Mrs. Dalrymple said when Judith reached her, to send a station wagon the next afternoon to pick up poor Mrs. Grenville's things.

Because she knew it would be hard to find parking space in crowded Soho, Judith drove her car a few hours later only as far as the Hampton Court railroad station. When she emerged from London's Waterloo Station she took a bus to Piccadilly and then threaded her way through Soho's network of narrow streets to Rocco's. One look around her after she walked in showed her that the restaurant was large and attractive, with fresh flowers on the white-clothed tables and pleasant oil landscapes on the walls. She also saw that Diana Sherill had not yet arrived.

As she waited at a small table, Judith looked around at the other patrons—a few well-dressed couples, several groups of what doubtless were business men, an all-feminine gathering that might have been some suburban garden club in town for the day, and one party which consisted of a man and woman in their forties and eight girls in their early teens. As Judith watched a waiter brought a candlelit cake to the table and, while the others sang "Happy Birthday," set it down before one of the girls.

Judith felt an amused wonder. Papa and Mama celebrating their young daughter's birthday by taking her and seven of her little friends to lunch. What could be more respectable? And yet to reach Rocco's that group must have driven, or walked, past porno bookstores, striptease joints with photographs of naked women in the windows, and shabby walkup apartment-hotels with rows of push buttons beside their outer doorways, each button surmounted by a card printed with some such name as Miss Kitty L'Amour or Miss Fanny D. Hill. Only the unflappable British would find it not in the least disturbing that the city's raunchiest neighborhood should also hold restaurants serving good food and attracting the most respectable of patrons.

Diana Sherill was threading her way through the tables now, wearing a pink linen suit and looking a few pounds heavier than she had the previous summer. She dropped into the chair opposite Judith.

"Oh, it's so good to see you, Judy. I'm sorry I'm late. At the last minute I found I didn't have a single pair of panty hose without runs. I had to nip out to Selfridge's —that's the nearest store to our apartment—and buy a pair. How are you, Judy? You're looking splendid."

"So are you."

Diana made a face. "I'm fat as a pig. Have you ordered yet? Anything to drink, I mean?"

"I was waiting for you."

"I think I'll have a martini, an American-style martini. The bartender here knows how to make them."

Judith felt surprise. Last summer she had never known Diana to drink anything stronger than white wine. Already the blond girl had signaled the waiter. He took their order for one American martini and one Campari and soda. After he had gone Diana said, "Don't you think this is a nice restaurant?"

"Very. How did you find it?"

"George found it. One day I was looking in his desk for stamps and I saw several matchbooks with 'Rocco's' printed on them. I asked him about it and he said that he'd had lunch here a few times with other men from the Department of the Environment. So one day last summer I had lunch here with Dulcie Craig. You remember her, don't you?"

"Yes, I remember her. Diana, what was it you wanted to see me about?"

Diana gave a nervous-sounding laugh. "Oh, Judith! Don't be in such a rush. Tell me about yourself first. I gather you didn't marry that writer."

Judith answered, in a constrained voice, "No, we didn't get married."

"But George tells me that you're here to illustrate another book by—what was his name? Barney something?" Judith nodded. "Does that mean you still may get married?"

"We might."

"Oh, here are our drinks." A moment later she said, lifting her glass, "Cheers." When she had set the drink down she went on, "Well, I guess if a girl has a real career, if she's an artist or something, marriage isn't so important to her. You know what? I'm taking painting lessons. Not that I have any hopes of becoming an artist. But it's fun, and it helps to fill up the day."

She chattered on through her first martini. When the waiter approached, menu in hand, she said, "Let's have another drink while we're waiting for our food."

"I haven't finished mine yet, but you go ahead."

The waiter took their order for one martini and two portions of veal with marsala sauce. By the time he returned to place their food before them and take away the empty glasses, Diana's voice was a trifle slurred. After she had eaten only a few mouthfuls of veal she laid down her fork and said, "Judith, do you know who killed Cecily Grenville?"

Startled by the question, and disconcerted by the intensity in Diana's rather prominent blue eyes, Judith said, "Of course I don't know. If I'd known I would have told the police."

"Well, perhaps you don't actually *know.* But you were her cousin, and you were practically living in the same house with her last summer. Surely you must have an idea who did it."

"I don't! If the police don't know, how could I?"

Diana ignored that. "I'll bet you think it was Steven, don't you? Lord knows she gave him enough reasons for killing her. And never mind that alibi of his. He could have hired someone. Don't you agree with me?"

There was fear, Judith realized now, in Diana's face and voice. What was she afraid of? Suddenly Judith felt almost sure of the answer. Diana was afraid that someone else, not Steven, had killed Cecily Grenville. And she had hoped to allay that fear by hearing Judith say that yes, she too was sure that Steven was responsible for his wife's death.

Diana said almost feverishly, "You know what they say. You're supposed to ask yourself *cui bono,* who benefits. And Steven's the only one who benefited from Cee-cee's death. That house is worth a packet. And she probably left him a lot more in cash and bonds and so forth."

75

Judith stiffened. To her surprise she found herself indignant at the suggestion that Steven might have killed his wife, not out of rage over her promiscuity and her constant taunting of him, but out of greed. "I doubt that. What with her gambling, and treating a dozen friends at a time to a week in the Greek isles, she couldn't have kept much of what her father left her. Besides, Steven doesn't live like a rich man. He goes to his office every day."

"That could be just a blind. He knows the police must still suspect him, even though they haven't been able to prove anything, and so he's going to wait a couple of years before he risks drawing attention to himself by spending a lot of money."

Sorry as she was for Diana's agitation, Judith also felt distinctly impatient with her. "Diana, do you really believe that a man who killed his wife for her money, and got away with it, would wait two years to start spending that money?"

"Well, then maybe he did it just because he hated her."

"And maybe someone else did it. That could easily be, considering the people she went around with. Most of them were pretty tacky. Some of them may even have been pushing drugs. But you know that. Even though she was my cousin, you and George knew her before I did. In fact, she mentioned to me once that she'd met George only a few weeks after she and Steven were married. Because they had some matters to talk over, Steven brought George home to lunch one day."

Diana's face flushed and then turned white. "Are you suggesting that George was one of Cecily's men?"

"Diana! Did I say anything like—"

"Because if you are, you couldn't be more wrong! George loves me too much to run after other women, especially a tramp like Cecily Grenville!"

Now Judith was convinced of the nature of Diana's

fears. She feared that her husband did *not* love her that much. She feared that he had been one of Cecily's bed partners. And she even feared that it was George who had brought the blade down on the sleeping girl—

Judith said, "Please, Diana. Think back over what I said. Did I say anything that implied that George and Cecily were anything more than friends?"

The other girl's voice sounded suddenly dull. "No, I don't suppose you did. Probably I shouldn't have had that second drink. Martinis make me—say things. And I really feel a little sick."

She reached into her shoulder bag, took out her wallet, and placed a bank note beside her plate. "That should cover lunch and the tip. No, I insist! I asked *you*, remember, so I'm paying. But you stay here and give the money to the waiter." She shoved back her chair. "I think I'd better leave now."

"If you're not feeling well, I should come with you."

"No! I want to be by myself. You stay here. Have some coffee." With Judith's concerned but baffled gaze following her, she moved a bit unsteadily to the café's entrance.

8

JUDITH DID have coffee. By the time she left the restaurant there was no sign of Diana on the street. Judith moved down the sidewalk slanting toward Piccadilly Circus, past a tea importer's office and a greengrocer's, past the gay bars and nudie clubs, many of them in buildings that, two hundred years ago, had been residences of the rich and fashionable.

A short, stout woman turning away from a chemist's window bumped shoulders with Judith. "I'm sorry," Judith said automatically, and then realized that the woman stood frozen, her face white in its frame of dyed red hair.

The woman said, "But you're—I thought you were—" Then relief came into her reddish-brown eyes. "Excuse me. I mistook you for someone else."

She hurried on up the sidewalk. Judith turned around in time to see her disappear inside a doorway. A small glass marquee projecting out above the doorstep bore the black lettered words, "Primrose Hotel."

Judith could guess the reason for the woman's terror. She must have thought that she had encountered Cecily Grenville's ghost in broad daylight. After a moment Judith walked back to the Primrose Hotel. On this warm day its front door stood open, revealing a dim hall and narrow stairs leading upward. She knew that in Soho there were hotels that rented rooms by the hour. She felt that this might be one of them.

According to Diana, George Sherill had said that he had lunched a few times in Soho with male colleagues. But what if instead it was Cecily he used to meet at that Greek Street restaurant? And what if, afterward, they used to visit this hotel—

Judith was sure it could not have been George—ambitious, rather pompous George—who had suggested coming to this place. It was the sort of kinky idea that would occur to a girl as sexually jaded as Cecily. Probably she had told him that it was the Primrose Hotel, or no place at all.

Judith stood motionless, only dimly aware of the pedestrians moving past her. If George, with his outwardly respectable air and his good government job, had been so desperately in love with Cecily that he would risk coming with her to this sort of hotel, then perhaps he had been desperate enough to write her that threatening letter. She hesitated a moment more and then went up the two shallow stone steps and into the hall. On a door at her left, painted a bilious green, black letters said, "Manager's Office."

Judith knocked. After a moment the door opened about eight inches and the red-haired woman peered out. "Yes?"

"May I talk to you for a moment?"

"I'm busy right now," the woman said, and started to close the door.

Judith said quickly, "It's about my cousin, Cecily Grenville. A moment ago you thought I was her, didn't you?"

Down the hall a door opened and closed. Footsteps approached. The woman said hurriedly, opening the door wider, "All right. Come in."

The room, although ugly, was clean and neat, even prim. A new-looking fake oriental rug in garish reds and blues. Dark blue overstuffed furniture with pink tatted antimacassars protecting the backs and arms. A cabinet television set bearing a colored photograph of two boys of about five and six, probably the woman's grandchildren.

"Sit down," the woman said, indicating one of the armchairs. She herself sat down on the sofa. Judith said, "My cousin used to come to your hotel with some man, didn't she?"

The woman said uneasily, "Look, Miss—"

"Dunne. Judith Dunne."

"What if I say yes? You're not going to tell the police she used to come here, are you? Her coming here doesn't mean I had anything to do with her getting murdered. And I don't want the police nosing around. I've never had any trouble with them, and I'd like to keep it that way."

"No, I won't tell the police." After Cecily's death the police and everyone else had learned enough scandalous details about her life. Why reveal more of them for no good reason?

The woman said, "Well, then, I'll tell you how it was. By the way, my name is Jergens, Alice Jergens." Judith nodded an acknowledgment. The woman went on, "Yes, she came here with a man four or perhaps five different afternoons. That was in March and April a year ago. Not that I knew who she was, not until I saw her picture in the paper after she was murdered. They'd told me their name was Grundy."

Mr. and Mrs. Grundy. No doubt that little joke had been Cecily's. "What did the man look like?"

"A very respectable type. Dark suits, public school tie. Brown hair and eyes. He looked as if he kept himself in good shape, but his hair was getting thin."

George Sherill, undoubtedly.

"But I don't think that there's a chance in the world that this man killed her," Mrs. Jergens said. "He looked to me like the kind who's planning to end up on the Queen's Honors List. He didn't seem the type to bring a woman to a place like this, let alone kill her."

But his possible motive for murder, Judith reflected, could have been rooted in that very ambition and respectability. He had risked both by bringing Cecily here, or rather, by letting her bring him here. For her sake he had endangered his whole future. And she had not rewarded him with even a pretense of fidelity. Such behavior could drive almost any man to violence.

Mrs. Jergens said, "You're sure you're not going to tell the police about your cousin coming to my place? Not that I've got anything to hide, you understand. It's just that if words gets around that the police have been calling on me— Well, it's bad for business."

"No, I won't tell the police."

But she would deliver that letter to them, as soon as she could return to her apartment and take it from where she had placed it, in the drawer of the nightstand beside her bed. She should have taken the letter to the police as soon as she found it. She had no right to suppress evidence. And a threatening letter, found among the effects of a woman who had been murdered, was certainly evidence.

She rose. "I must leave now. Thank you, Mrs. Jergens."

9

More than two hours later she sat in the Hampton Court Village police station. It had taken her that long to travel—by bus and train and her rented car—from Soho to her apartment and then back to the village.

The white-haired, ruddy-faced man across the desk from her was reading for the second time that badly typed letter, holding it gingerly by its upper corners. Now he laid it down on his desk. Judith had not realized that veteran policemen could look embarrassed, but this one did. Perhaps what had disconcerted him was the letter's reference to the photographer who also liked boys.

"You did right to bring this to us, Miss Dunne. We'll turn it over to the C.I.D. I doubt that they'll be able to trace it, though. They're not apt to find the writer's fingerprints, not clear ones, anyway, because it's been handled by at least two other people, your cousin and you."

"But you think that the person who wrote that letter may have been the one who—who killed her?"

"That could be, or it could have been someone else entirely." Again he looked somewhat embarrassed. "Evidently Mrs. Grenville's way of life was what might be called dangerous."

"I know," Judith said, and stood up.

He too got to his feet. "Thank you again, Miss Dunne. And if you find anything else of significance among Mrs. Grenville's belongings, please let us know."

She drove to The Columns down a road deep in the shadow of its bordering trees. After unlocking the gate she glanced at her watch. Already almost six. Just the same, she would try to finish packing Cecily's things before going up to her apartment. She relocked the gate and then drove to the corner of the main house and got out. For a moment she looked at the north wall. The man named Clancy had removed the wisteria vine entirely now, but it had left its ghostly outline in the form of darker bricks, protected by the vine for so many years from the fading effects of the sun. She turned and walked to the front door.

George Sherill sat at his desk, knowing that he should go home, and yet unwilling to. The room seemed far too quiet. Helen, his secretary, had left an hour ago, looking more than a little miffed because he had ignored her hint that he could take her to dinner if he liked. Now that it was six o'clock, the tourists too had been shepherded by the guards from the massive building, although no doubt some of them still strolled about the palace grounds.

He had more to worry about now than what Diana and the Dunne girl might have said to each other over the luncheon table. Two hours ago he had gone over to the palace's outdoor restaurant. As often happened Mrs. Dalrymple, a veritable fountain of good works, was there, treating her fellow members of the Missionary Society to tea. As he started past her table with a polite nod, she put an arresting hand on his arm. "Oh, Mr. Sherill, guess who I heard from this morning. Judith Dunne, that American girl who used to be sketching here at the palace last summer."

His nerves tightened. He said, still smiling, "She called you?"

"Yes, she's packing up her cousin's clothing to donate it to the church. Naturally I was a little shocked at the thought of our receiving Cecily Grenville's clothing." She looked shocked, pleasantly so. "One heard so many horrifying things about her, even before her death but especially afterward. Her clothing will be sold in a good cause, though. And the poor thing certainly paid for her behavior, didn't she?"

"That's right," George had said, and turned away from the counter to where a sullen-looking fat girl dispensed tea from an urn.

Now he stared at the closed door, thinking of the electric typewriter in the outer office. Late one afternoon last summer after his secretary—his former secretary—had gone home, he had sat at that typewriter. Half out of his mind with rage and pain and jealousy, he had tapped out a letter with his index fingers, taken it back to London with him, and mailed it to Cecily that night.

Thank God he'd had sense enough not to write it in longhand, or to sign it. Still, paper could hold fingerprints, which could be traced. And typed material could be traced to a particular machine. Again and again late last summer and early fall he had thought of trying to get rid of that typewriter, even though it was government property. But the only way he could think of to accomplish that was to damage the machine so severely that it would have to be replaced. And that would have meant awkward questions, perhaps not just from the palace administration. Already the police were aware that he knew Cecily, and they had subjected him to a routine questioning. Their interview with him, he felt sure, had been no more searching than those they had conducted with dozens of others. But if they had found the letter, and if they somehow heard of a mishap to his typewriter—

In a way it would be comforting to think of the letter as being in the hands of the police. If they had it, and had not traced it to him after all these months, then probably they never would. But what if it was still in the Grenville house, hidden somewhere that only another woman would think to look? What if Cecily's cousin, going through everything with a fine-toothed comb for that frigging Missionary Society, found the letter and turned it over to the police?

Damn that American girl, he thought. If only she had stayed on her own side of the Atlantic.

In the big silent house Judith continued to pack the gold-colored sandals, costume jewelry, and gauzy scarves which had accented the beauty of a girl now ten months dead. There had been no need to go to the attic for more containers. Several of the hat boxes on the closet shelf had proved to be empty. In them she had placed such hard-to-classify articles as a set of electric hair curlers she had found on the floor at one end of the closet and a box of monogrammed notepaper from the small desk in one corner of the room.

Finally she looked around her. Cartons and hat boxes, all crammed with Cecily's belongings, sat on the white rug. Wads of tissue paper, which had just been taking up space in the hat boxes, were strewn over the fireplace's floor where she had tossed them. When she left she would take the paper with her and deposit it in the covered trash bin under the stairs leading up to the carriage-house apartment. She felt sure that her cousin would have approved of the now-empty shelves and drawers in this room. No matter what else she was, Cecily had been generous to a fault. She would much prefer that her expensive garments please other women, rather than serve no purpose at all.

She heard a noise, a sustained rolling sound from somewhere overhead. It grew louder by the second. A jet plane. But now that it was closer she realized that its sound was different from that of other jets. It was not a roar, but a diffused rumble, like that of some huge freight train in the sky. After a moment she realized that it must be the supersonic Concorde, on its glide path to Heathrow Airport.

The rumbling dwindled away. In the near-silence she became aware of another sound. It was a dry, rattling noise that suggested a stream of fine gravel. She turned and looked at the long-unused fireplace in time to see the last few particles of some whitish substance fall from the fireplace chimney onto the crumpled tissue paper.

She realized what must have happened. The plane's heavy vibration had shaken grains of dry, disintegrated mortar from between some of the bricks forming the fireplace's rear wall. Curious to see if she was right, she crossed to the fireplace, knelt on the white brick apron, and looked up. Yes, around each of two adjoining bricks there was a narrow, almost imperceptible space, appearing like a thin dark line, where mortar had been. But why had mortar fallen away from around those two bricks and no others?

The answer came to her, speeding her heartbeats. All that mortar had not fallen out. It had been dug out. The few grains she had heard rattling down were some of those left behind after the two bricks had been chiseled loose.

Once more she felt almost sure that there had been an intruder in this room two nights before. Oh, perhaps he hadn't chiseled out the mortar from around those bricks, at least not then. But perhaps he had known the bricks

86

could be removed, thus creating a place where objects such as a candle might be hidden—

She got up, took a nail file from her shoulder bag, and again knelt on the hearth. With the file she found it easy to maneuver one brick and then the other far enough out from the fireplace wall that she could grasp it. She laid both bricks beside her on the hearth. Then, a bit hesitantly, she reached up into the small cavern created by the bricks' removal. Yes, something in there. But maybe after all she'd been wrong about seeing candle light. Or perhaps the prowler had taken the candle away with him. Anyway, the object her fingers had found felt neither like a candle nor a candle holder. Instead it seemed to be something about six inches long, made of smooth wood.

She drew it out and then, with a strangled cry, let it fall onto the mounds of tissue paper. Momentarily paralyzed, she stared down at the brown wooden handle and wide steel blade.

The cleaver. Seconds ago she had held in her hand the weapon that had severed Cecily's spinal cord.

So it was not, as the police had thought, at the bottom of the Thames. Someone had hidden it here, someone who perhaps came back here at night now and then to relive what he had done to Cecily. She could imagine that faceless someone removing the cleaver from its hiding place and then carrying it over to the empty floor space where the bed had once stood. She had a sickening vision of him—a smile on his lips, eyes ashine in the candlelight—chopping downward with the cleaver again and again. Now, with the light fading in this silent house, she could almost hear the drawn-out swish, swish, swish of that broad blade cutting through the air.

The paralysis dropped from her. She got to her feet. She snatched up her shoulder bag from the chaise longue and raced down through the thickening shadows and out the front door.

In her apartment, as soon as she had locked and bolted her door, she called the police. Then she went into the bedroom and crammed a nightgown and summer-weight yellow robe into her flight bag.

She would unlock the gate for the police and take them up to the room where that hideous thing lay, but when they drove away, so would she. She could not spend the night here, not if there was the remotest chance that he might come back, that someone she had pictured wielding the cleaver there in the candlelight.

10

THE SOUND of rain awoke her. For a moment she looked with puzzled eyes at the other single bed, a twin to the one in which she lay, and at a wall hung with green-and-yellow striped wallpaper and prints of red-coated hunters and long-eared hounds. Then she remembered. This was the Ivy Hotel in Hampton Court Village.

The night before she had waited outside the gates until two policemen, both in their late twenties, drove up to The Columns. She had led them into the shadowy house and up to where lingering daylight still came through the windows of that corner room.

For a few moments the men had looked down silently at the cleaver resting on the crumpled tissue paper. Then the taller of them, a red-haired man with a slight brogue, knelt on the hearth. Not touching the cleaver, he shone a flashlight he had brought from the police car with him down onto the gleaming blade. "Bloke must have washed it. It looks clean as a whistle. Still, perhaps there's a bit of dried blood up under the handle. And there's always a chance of fingerprints."

He shone the flashlight up into the mouth of the opening in the fireplace's rear wall. Then he laid the flashlight aside and thrust his hand into the small cavern. "Nothing else in there," he said after a moment, and got to his feet.

Judith said, "Those bricks were chiseled loose, weren't they?"

"Must have been, miss." He was dusting the knees of his trousers with his hands.

"Do—do you think he did it the night he killed her?"

"Isn't likely, is it, miss? After a bloke had done a thing like that, he wouldn't stay messing about with fireplaces. My guess is that hiding place was there before he killed her. He knew about it, and decided to use it for the cleaver."

The killer knew about it. That meant he could not have been some casual intruder. Almost surely he had been someone so thoroughly familiar with this room that he even knew about that concealed hiding place.

The other policeman, a stocky young man with a formidable blond mustache, said, "Daft thing to do, leaving the weapon here. Why didn't he take it away with him?"

His partner said, "Of course, we can't be sure it is the weapon. That's for the lab men to say."

Judith realized that this was only a *pro forma* statement, perhaps made to impress a somewhat younger colleague. Surely there could be little doubt about the cleaver. The police had already determined, from the nature of Cecily's wounds, what sort of blade had inflicted them. The chances were overwhelming that a weapon of that description, concealed only a few feet from where she had died, was the one which had killed her.

The red-haired policeman crouched, put both hands under the tissue paper on which the cleaver rested, and carefully folded the paper over the knife. With the paper-wrapped cleaver in his hands he straightened and said, "The lab people will tend to this right away. And we'll be in touch with you, miss."

"Wait! I'd like to follow you into the village. I don't want to stay here tonight."

The tall policeman looked through the rear window at the carriage house, so close to this room. "Can't say that I blame you. It must have been a nasty shock, finding that thing in your hand. All right, miss. We'll wait for you."

She had followed the police car into the village and then driven up and down its high street. Even though it was past nine by then, enough of the long summer twilight remained so that she could see that there was no "bed-sitting room" sign in the window of the house where she had stayed for two weeks last year. No similar signs were in the windows or on the lawns of other houses. Finally she drove to the hotel. The price quoted by the room clerk shocked her into momentary speechlessness. Twenty-two pounds, almost forty dollars, per night. No, he told her, he knew of no private houses with vacant rooms to rent. England had so many visitors this summer that accommodations in and around London were scarce indeed.

Now she got out of bed and walked over to the window. Rain streamed down the pane, so that the brick terrace with its metal chairs and tables and furled umbrellas two stories below seemed to waver. What was she going to do? She could not afford twenty-two pounds a day, or even a fraction of that, just to keep a roof over her head. Would she have to go back to New York before her work here was even well started?

Or could she bring herself to go on staying in that carriage-house apartment? She found the prospect less daunting than it had seemed the night before. After all, her discovery of that cleaver made the situation no more dangerous than it had been earlier, because it was most unlikely that the person who had hidden it would know that she had found it. The wisteria vine, his probable means of entrance to that room, was gone now. And the police would not publicize the finding of the weapon, not unless or until they made an arrest.

Yes, if she could just curb her imagination, she could go on staying there, trusting in her double-locked door, her gun beside her bed, and the phone which could bring a police car there within minutes. As for right now, she would drive to the apartment, pick up her drawing case, and try to distract herself with several hours of hard work at the palace.

But first, she decided grimly, she would phone down to the desk and ask for breakfast to be sent up, even though she had little appetite for it. After all, breakfast was included in the room rate, and at these prices she was not going to pass up anything coming to her.

Rain was still falling gently when, nearly an hour later, she unlocked the wrought-iron gates and drove back past The Columns to the carriage-house stairs. The rooms looked gloomy in the gray light, so much so that even though she was determined to go on living here, she felt a need right now to be on her way to the palace as soon as possible. She left the flight bag, still packed, on a chair in the bedroom, picked up her sketching case from where it leaned against the wall in the living room, and walked down the short hall toward the front door.

It wasn't until then that she saw the folded piece of paper lying on the floorboards just inside the door. Had it been there when she entered the apartment only moments ago? Yes, undoubtedly. She could see the stain her rain-wet shoe had made when she stepped on the paper's edge. With an odd, premonitory chill running down her spine, she set down her sketching case, picked up the piece of paper and unfolded it.

Words printed crudely in pencil seemed to leap up at her:

> Annie and Cee-cee and Miss Judith Dunne
> Think they are three but to me are all one
> I keep a count as Death scythes down the row:
> Two of them down and one left to go.

A thin line of hardened glue clung to the top of the sheet. Evidently it had been torn from the sort of writing tablet available at any Woolworth's. With a cold sickness in the pit of her stomach Judith thrust her free hand against the wall to steady herself and read the bit of doggerel through again. For her it conjured up the image of a hooded figure, swinging a scythe down a row, not of golden heads of wheat, but human heads. She sensed a dark glee as well as hatred behind those lines.

And who was Annie?

A few sentences from Cecily's letter of more than a year ago leaped into her mind. "Sorry not to have answered sooner, but we've had a bit of an upset here. A girl named Annette Swayle was killed here in the village two weeks ago. She worked for us whenever we needed extra help. In fact, Steven had given her a lift home only a few hours before her body was found, and so as you can imagine the police were asking a lot of questions."

The police. She must take this hideous little rhyme to them right away.

She thrust the piece of cheap paper into her shoulder bag, picked up her sketching case, and moved out onto the small landing, almost unaware of the gently falling rain. She locked the door and then, hand clinging to the rail, went down the rain-slippery steps. She backed and turned her car, drove to the gate, and locked it with hands made clumsy by agitation.

She was almost a quarter of a mile from the house when she saw the dark green Mercedes coming toward her along the narrow road. Steven's car. What was he doing here at this early hour? Steven, who hated his wife, and who had given a day-worker named Annette Swayle a ride home a few hours before her death.

And then she realized something else about Steven. Except for Cecily herself, there was no one more likely to know about those removable bricks in the fireplace.

Her hands tightened on the wheel. He was passing her now. He called out something, but she could not hear the words through the drumming of blood in her ears. She stretched her lips into what she knew must look like the parody of a smile, and drove on.

After a moment she looked into the rear view mirror and saw with a leap of her heart that he had made a U-turn and was coming after her. She pressed harder on the accelerator, but even as the Volvo leaped forward she knew it would be no match for the powerful Mercedes. And there was no other car in sight along the tree-lined road in either direction.

He was alongside her now, gesturing for her to pull over to the side of the road. With panic surging through her, she tried to press even harder on the throttle. The Mercedes, drawing ahead, began to angle toward the left, as if to block her path. Instinctively she swerved off the road. In the tall grass the Volvo coughed and died.

She heard a car door slam. He was striding toward her, anger in his face. She thought of that gun resting uselessly in the nightstand drawer.

He jerked the car door open. "What the hell's the matter with you?" When she did not answer but just stared at him, hands gripping the wheel, he got into the car beside her and closed the door. "Well?"

Raindrops on the windshield cast blotchy shadows on

his face. She knew there must be similar shadows on her own face. She asked thinly, "Where were you going?"

"On this road, where would I be going? To my house, of course. Is there anything in that to send you into a panic?"

"It's just that—So early in the day—"

"When I went up into the attic to get those cartons day before yesterday I saw that the roof had been leaking. I had nothing really important to do this morning, so I decided to drive out for another look."

"But why—"

"Why did I come after you? When I passed you I could tell by your face that something was wrong, and so I turned around. When you tried to outrun me I knew that something was very wrong. Now what is it?"

She looked at him, considering. If he were the one who had slipped that folded piece of paper under her door sometime during the night, then of course he already knew about it, and there was no point in withholding the information. And if he hadn't composed that grotesque little jingle, perhaps he should know that someone else had. She reached into her shoulder bag, brought out the sheet of paper, and handed it to him.

He looked at it for perhaps twenty seconds and then said quietly, "My God." He extended the paper to her. "Put it back in your purse. We'll take it to the police. Now where did you find it?"

She told him. "That—that Annie in the verse. Who do you think he meant?"

His fingers drummed on the dashboard's curved top. "There was a local girl named Annette Swayle. I believe some people called her Annie. Anyway, she was killed last spring. Months later—around last Christmas, in fact —a man who had been sent to prison on another charge got in a fight with a fellow inmate and was fatally wounded. As he was dying, he confessed to killing the Swayle girl. But up until then the police didn't have a clue. For awhile they even pestered Cecily and me because the girl had frequently worked for us. In fact that very afternoon, only a few hours before her death, I had driven her home—"

He broke off, and then said harshly, "I see it now. You knew about the Swayle girl. Cecily must have written you or told you later on about the police questioning me. And so this morning you thought that I was the one who had put that paper under your door."

She looked at him silently, knowing that denial would be useless, knowing that the truth must show in her face. His hands shot out and grasped her shoulders. "Now you listen to me! I came to hate my wife, but I didn't kill her, nor did I hire anyone to kill her. Oh, yes, I know that people have been saying that sort of thing. And I didn't kill the Swayle girl, either. I've never killed anyone." He gave her shoulders a shake. "Can't you get that through your thick head?"

She was still afraid of him, and the harshness in his face and voice did nothing to allay that fear. Nevertheless she managed to keep her voice steady. "You've tried to get me to leave. Oh, you didn't take any legal steps to keep me out of that apartment, but you've made it plain you find me unwelcome."

"And you thought that was because of my guilty conscience. Everytime I saw you I was reminded of what I'd done to Cecily. Is that it?"

"It could have been."

"Well, it hasn't been. Oh, not that you don't remind me of her. You're so like her in looks, and so unlike her in every other way." She saw his face change. "That bothered me last summer, bothered me like the very devil, and it bothers me now."

His hands still gripped her shoulders. Motionless, he looked at her for a long moment. She felt her heartbeats quicken, partly with fear, partly with an excitement she did not want to define.

Then he released her, moved over to the far corner of the seat, and stared through the rain-dotted windshield. Heartbeats still fast, she waited for him to say, "Sorry I was rough with you."

Instead he said, after perhaps half a minute, "Why don't you go home?"

Her anger flared, stronger than her fear. "Why should I?"

"Because you're afraid here, and apparently with good reason. And because you should never have come here in the first place, not even last summer." He paused. "Did you ever read Henry James? *Daisy Miller* in particular?"

She said coldly, "I have not."

"It's about an encounter between Old World corruption and American innocence, with innocence getting the worst of it. And you Americans still tend to be innocent—or perhaps unwary is a better word. Anyway, you shouldn't have come here last summer. And certainly you shouldn't have returned this summer. I was amazed that you would be willing to spend more weeks in that apartment, only a few yards from where Cecily died."

Now he was calling her insensitive. She answered, in a shaken voice, "I had my reasons. I have a book to illustrate. And I don't have much money to support myself while I'm doing it."

"But why did you choose to do that particular book?" When she didn't answer he said, "It's because you're in love with the man writing the book, isn't it?" As her face swung toward him he added, "Oh yes, Cecily told me about it. She said you intended to marry him. How is it that you haven't?"

She felt her face flush. "Perhaps we will marry when I return to New York in the fall. Anyway, isn't that my business?"

"Of course. But let someone who's been through that particular mill give you a bit of advice. Don't cling to an exploitative person just because you feel committed to him. If you do you'll end up hating that person, which is bad, or you'll find yourself a broken creature with no self-respect, which is worse."

She didn't answer. After a moment he said, "Well, if you insist upon staying, I'm going to see to it that there will be no one prowling around that place in the future." He opened the car door. "I'll lead the way to the police station."

"Wait! First I'd better tell you that I saw the police twice yesterday."

He asked sharply, "Why?"

"Well, first I took them a letter I'd found—"

As she told him about that jealous, pleading, desperate letter, she kept her gaze fixed on his face, hoping to learn from his reaction whether or not he had known of the letter's existence. But his expression, stony now, told her nothing.

Finally she said, "Do you have any idea who could have written it?"

"No definite idea." He gave a short laugh. "Although I can think of about a dozen possibilities. Now you said you saw the police twice."

"Yes. After I'd finished packing Cecily's things early yesterday evening, I—I found the cleaver that must have killed her."

"You *what?*" The astonishment in his face appeared to be completely genuine.

When she had finished telling him about her unnerving discovery and about the visit from the two policemen, she asked, "Did you know about those loose bricks in the fireplace?"

He shook his head. "If the fireplaces in the house had been in use, I of course would have checked them from time to time. But open fires had been outlawed even before Cecily's father bought the house for her."

"Do you have any idea of what Cecily might have kept hidden there? Jewelry, perhaps?"

"Not Cecily. She paid out fortunes in insurance premiums just so she wouldn't have to worry about her jewelry being stolen."

"What, then?"

Again he gave that short laugh. "Uppers. Downers. Maybe cocaine. She was as free-handed with drugs as with anything else, but she didn't like discovering every now and then that her friends had cleaned her out entirely. My guess is she chiseled out those bricks so that she could keep a private supply safe in her room.

"All right," he added, stepping out onto the grass, "let's call on the police."

Around four in the afternoon she drove back along that same tree-lined road. For a day that had begun so grimly, it had turned out fairly well. At the police station she and Steven had been shown into the office of the same gray-haired official she had seen the afternoon before. Obviously the policeman was far more disturbed by that ugly little quatrain than he had been by a letter written almost a year earlier.

"You can rest assured," he said, "that the C.I.D. will give their attention to this right away."

Steven asked, "Do you remember the death of that Swayle girl early last spring? My wife and I called her Annette, but I believe some people called her Annie."

"That they did, sir. And of course I remember her."

A constrained note in his voice indicated that he remembered also that Steven had been questioned about the girl's death. "An old lag in Dartmoor last winter confessed to the crime just before he died. He'd been imprisoned for something far less serious. Smash-and-grab, I think it was."

"But don't you think that Annie"—Steven gestured at the sheet of cheap paper lying on the desk—"refers to Annette Swayle?"

"I can't think of anyone else it would mean, sir. I've been here twenty-five years and in all that time there's not been another local murder victim with a name like Annie, or anything near it. Looks as if the joker who wrote that bit of verse wants to make himself out even more dangerous than he probably is."

"Either that," Steven said, "or the man in Dartmoor made a false confession. That happens, doesn't it?"

"Sometimes. Of course it's a sick thing to do. But then, some authorities complain that most criminals are sick in the head. But about you, Miss Dunne. I don't think you should go on staying there in an empty apartment behind a vacant house, with no neighbor nearer than a quarter of a mile."

"Don't worry." Steven's voice was grim. "That house is going to have tenants right away. Today, in fact. Now about that cleaver Miss Dunne found yesterday evening."

"The C.I.D. has it now, sir. We should get a report on it within a few days at most. Incidentally, a C.I.D. man will be here sometime before noon. He wants to take a look at that fireplace. I intended to phone you at your office to see if you, as the house's owner, would be able to go out there and let him in."

"I'll be available. In fact, since I intend to rent the house, it would be best if he finished his inspection as quickly as possible." He paused. "About that fireplace. It seems strange that the police didn't look at it closely enough to find that cleaver."

"You might think so, sir. But consider this. The fact that the mortar was missing from around a couple of the bricks up inside the fireplace was unnoticeable unless something drew it to someone's attention, as happened with Miss Dunne here. And another thing. You expect a murderer to take his weapon away and get rid of it, or, if he's in a panic, drop it at the scene of the crime and then run. What you don't expect him to do was what this joker did—wash off the weapon and then hide it only a few feet away from the victim. Do you see my point, sir?"

"Yes, I suppose I do. Well, if there is nothing more, I'll leave now." He shook hands with the gray-haired man, nodded to Judith, and walked out. She lingered for a moment more to thank the constable. When she emerged onto the sidewalk the Mercedes was not in sight.

Judith drove to the palace then. In a stone-floored room off-limits to the tourists moving through the newer parts of the vast structure she set up her easel. Soon she had managed to become absorbed in the first of her illustrations for Barney's chapter on Charles the First, whose honeymoon battles with his fifteen-year-old French bride had scandalized not only the English court but that of the young queen's mother, Maria de Medici. Judith depicted the enraged bride, a small girl with large black eyes and an abundance of black curls, sobbing as she clung to the metal frame of a casement window whose panes she had just smashed with her fists. King Charles, almost as young and almost as small as his wife, was also in the sketch, trying to pry her scratched and bloodied hands loose from the window.

Judith was glad that Barney had agreed to several

more illustrations featuring Charles and his wife. She planned to depict stages of their life at Hampton Court after they began to fall in love, a love so deep that it had lasted through the birth of nine children and right up to the time of Charles's death on the headsman's block.

At four o'clock she drove out of the palace grounds, back through the village, and along the road toward The Columns. As she neared the house some of her anxiety returned. He would acquire a tenant, Steven had promised grimly, that very day. But what sort of a tenant could he persuade to move in on such short notice? Some elderly pensioner, living in a furnished room somewhere, who could carry most of his possessions in a suitcase? Or had Steven decided to reoccupy the house himself? The idea brought her a strange mingling of excitement and fear.

She could see now that the gates stood open. She drove through and then abruptly stopped the car. Coming toward her through the knee-high grass was a sit-down lawn mower, piloted by a deeply tanned man of about twenty-five with shoulder-length blond hair. Except for ragged khaki shorts and a string of amber beads, he was naked.

He stopped the mower and walked over to the Volvo. "You must be Miss Dunne. My name is Brother John. We rented this house from Mr. Grenville a few hours ago."

Judith felt dazed. "Brother who?"

"John. Our getting it seemed like a miracle. For weeks now we've been camping out two miles from here in a farmer's field, hoping that sooner or later we would hear of a big house we could afford to rent. Then today an estate agent in the village phoned the farmer. He said that Mr. Grenville might rent this place to us immediately if we'd drive over here and talk to him."

A young woman in an ankle-length brown dress, with blond braids falling over her shoulders, approached through the long grass. She held a diapered baby on one hip. By the other hand she led a little girl of about three, who wore a dress as long as the woman's.

Brother John said, "This is Sister Esther, my wife. And these are our children, Deborah and John." Another young woman, red-haired and freckled and wearing an ankle-length green dress, also had approached the car. "This is Sister Naomi. Her husband, Brother Matthew, is helping Brother Paul move our things into the house through the back door."

Judith felt a little hysterical. "How many of you will be living here?"

"Well, let's see. There are seven adults and eight children."

"Nine children," his wife said. "You forget Brother Paul and Sister Martha's new baby."

"That's right. Nine children. Oh, by the way, a lady and two men from some missionary society were here about half an hour ago. They took some boxes away from upstairs in a station wagon. They told me to tell you."

"Thank you. You're all members of some religious group, aren't you?"

"Yes. We're the Children of Emmanuel."

"I see. Well, goodbye for now."

As she drove back to her apartment she reflected that Steven Grenville had indeed kept his promise to provide her with neighbors. She felt glad that no Hare Krishna people had been looking for a house in the neighborhood. Not that she hadn't rather enjoyed the sight of Hare Krishnas surging orange-robed and shaven-headed through New York subway cars. But chanting and tambourine-banging on the IRT was one thing. Having it right next door day after day would be quite another. She hoped that the Children of Emmanuel did not go in for chanting.

11

THE CHILDREN of Emmanuel did not. Except for Sunday mornings and Wednesday nights, when the faint strains of voices singing "Rock of Ages" or "Bringing in the Sheaves" reached her ears, the Children seemed as quiet as any ordinary household—quieter, in fact, because apparently the sect frowned upon radio and television.

Judith was pleased that now the lawn was kept mowed. She liked seeing, through the pulled-back draperies of Cecily's old room, that a loom had been set up where the chaise longue once stood. Glancing through her own window at that corner room, Judith often saw one or another of the long-gowned women working at the loom, although whether they were weaving a rug, or blanket, or material for clothing she could not tell.

Most of all, of course, she appreciated knowing that now it was highly unlikely that an intruder would enter the house or even the grounds.

Nevertheless, she realized that having numerous neighbors within earshot did not mean there was no longer any danger. Danger would continue as long as he was at large, that person who had killed Cecily and then —assuming it was the same one—had returned to visit by night that room with its hidden cleaver, and to climb an outside staircase to slip a grotesque rhyme under Judith's door. But although it might be illogical, now that she felt safe at night in her apartment she felt safer during the days too.

Her work went well. Sometimes she sat sketching beside a tree-bordered canal, with swans floating on its surface, where Charles the Second, so unlike his pious and domestic father, used to stroll with his ladies and his spaniels. Sometimes in the late afternoons, after the palace was closed to visitors, she sat sketching in the elaborate rooms—all lofty ceilings and carved marble fireplaces and gilt furniture—in the "new" part of the palace, that section designed by Christopher Wren almost two hundred years ago for William and Mary. Other times—not for Barney's book, but her own pleasure—she sketched the shadowy little courts in the oldest part of the palace, with their deeply worn flagstones and their lampposts that dated from the first Elizabeth's time.

Every now and then she saw George Sherill talking to one of the many guards who patroled the palace and its grounds, or personally escorting distinguished visitors through the various courts and corridors. Whenever he and Judith encountered each other he would greet her politely but distantly and then hurry on. She would look after him, thinking of that frowsy hotel in Soho, and of that unsigned letter she had found in Cecily's housecoat, and which he might or might not have written.

Diana Sherill came to Hampton Court a couple of times, and both times sought Judith out, once beside the Great Fountain Pool with its avenues of lime trees radiating from around it, and once in one of the brick-walled old gardens, fragrant with roses and loud with bee-hum, where once Henry the Eighth had tilted against other mounted men and, not surprisingly, had unseated all of them. Each time Judith had the feeling that Diana's visits were designed to counteract any unfortunate impression her behavior might have conveyed that day in Soho. For fifteen minutes or so before going to her husband's office, Diana chattered on about the bracelet George had given her for her birthday, and the trip to Rhodes he had promised her, and the sundry other generosities and indulgences which made her believe that hers was the best husband in the world. Embarrassed, Judith made responses that she hoped sounded properly admiring and impressed.

She began to see Steven Grenville, too, at the palace. The first time was three days after they had gone to the police station together. That afternoon as she sat sketching in the Pond Garden south of the palace, among the stocks and begonias and ageratum, she looked up and saw, with a tightening of her nerves, that Steven was walking toward her along a graveled path. He halted and said, "Who are you putting in this sketch? Poor old gout-crippled Queen Anne?"

Surprise held her silent for an instant. At no time since she'd known him had he treated her in this casually friendly manner. Was he, like Diana, trying to wipe out an earlier impression? Maybe he hoped that a display of what the English call mateyness would make her forget that he had seized her roughly by the shoulders and shaken her.

"Yes, this will be a sketch of Queen Anne. How did you guess?"

"I know this was one of her favorite spots. Are you aware that when she became too crippled to sit in a saddle she would hunt in a horse-drawn chaise, driving it herself? Can't you just see her in it, tearing around Bushey Park?"

Judith nodded. "Perhaps I'll draw her that way." That particular story had not been in Barney's book—after all, he could not crowd in everything—but perhaps if he liked the sketch he would add a paragraph about Queen Anne bumping across gullies and over wooden bridges in pursuit of a stag. She asked, "How is it you know these things?"

He countered, smiling, "Why is it that people think that engineers and architects are interested only in their specialties? I manage to gather information from a few other fields." He paused, and then asked abruptly, "How do you like your new neighbors?"

"I like them fine. But I should think you would be worried about the wear and tear on your house."

"Wear and tear! Do you know what some of Cecily's friends did one night? They brought a whole crateful of rabbits from somewhere and set them loose in the house. Then they brought in a pack of dogs and had a rabbit hunt, upsetting furniture, tearing down curtains, and smashing lamps. I wasn't there when it happened, but I saw what the place looked like the next day." He glanced at his watch. "Well, I'd better get to the business that brought me here."

"What business is that?"

"The *son et lumière* show that will be given here at the palace in a few weeks. I'll be going over every phase of the production with the engineers and so on to make sure that the building will suffer no architectural damage."

She echoed, puzzled, *"Son et lumière?"*

"Sound and lights. It's a kind of dramatization of the history of a building, and it is always given at night. The audience—they'll sit in a grandstand out beyond the west entrance to the palace—won't see any actors. Instead they will see lights and hear recorded voices. They will see a light, for instance, behind the window of what was once Catherine of Aragon's bedroom, and hear Cardinal Wolsey's voice pleading with her to give Henry the

Eighth a divorce. Then the audience will see moving lights, like torchlight, to the south of the palace where the trees slope down to the river, and hear the sound of a lute, and the king's voice wooing Anne Boleyn."

"It sounds wonderful."

"Yes, it's very effective. They presented it once before, several years ago. I think you'll enjoy it." Abruptly he changed the subject. "Another thing. The police called me at my office this morning about that—cleaver. I suppose they'll telephone you about it later today at your apartment. Anyway, the only prints they found on it were yours. Your fingerprints were taken last summer, you'll recall, along with those of anyone else who had access to that house and that room."

She nodded.

In a constrained voice he went on, "The police lab did find a minute trace of dried blood at one end of the blade, just where it fits into the handle. They tested it, and found that it matched Cecily's blood type."

"Then they are sure it's the one that—that—"

"That was used to kill her? Yes, they're sure. Well, I'll leave you to your work now." He turned and walked away.

Two days later, as she sat at a table of that outdoor restaurant with a cup of tea and one of those ninety-nine-percent bread sandwiches, Steven appeared beside her, a tea mug in his hand. "Mind if I join you?"

Again she felt that odd tightening of all her nerves. After a moment she said, "Please do."

He sat down. "You don't really like that, do you? English sandwiches don't have enough filling for one to even taste it."

"I'm getting used to them. And I should think you would be."

"Not I. I'll have lunch at the pub a few doors from my

office. The tea is just to tide me over."

"How are the sound and light show preparations going?"

"Well enough. We'll start installing the concealed loud speakers next week. How about your sketches?"

"I think I'm doing all right. I hope so."

He was silent for a long moment. Then he asked abruptly, almost as if against his will, "This writing chap in New York. What's he like?"

"It's hard to say what anyone is like. But he's twenty-seven, medium height, curly brown hair—"

"I mean, what do you two have in common besides work?" Again she had the impression that he asked the question against his own better judgment.

"Why, lots of things. We both like movies, and classical music as well as rock and jazz. We like taking long walks around New York and having picnic lunches in Central Park. While I set out the lunch, Barney flies his kite—"

"He *what?*"

Her voice became stiff. "He flies his kite. Kite flying is quite popular in America."

"You mean that grown men—"

"Yes, grown men! And if Americans are doing it now, the English will be doing it soon. You know how that is."

"Oh Lord, I suppose you're right." He fell silent, cup in hand, gaze fixed on her face. She had a feeling—half-hopeful, half-apprehensive—that he was about to say, "Let's have dinner together tonight." Instead he set down his cup and pushed back his chair, "Well, I'd best be going. I have things to do."

But if Steven's attitude toward her seemed ambivalent and George Sherill's downright cold, at least one man she knew from the previous summer was unfailingly pleasant. Wherever she set up her easel—down by the

Thames, in one of the many palace gardens, or along some vaulted corridor—she knew that Kyle Hodge was apt to appear to look at her work. His comments were always perceptive and sometimes even helpful. And she found his talk of Hampton Court Palace fascinating because he knew the sort of facts that only a professional historian bothers to dredge up—how much per hour Cardinal Wolsey paid his bricklayers, and how much beer from the palace brewery each lady in waiting was alloted in Henry the Eighth's time.

Twice Kyle took her to a pleasant pub across the road from the palace for a late afternoon drink. By the second afternoon Judith felt she knew him well enough to ask the question she had not asked that day they met at the Tower of London. "How is it that you'll be teaching at a new school next term?"

He smiled. "You might say we had a bit of class warfare at my old school, and I was one of the casualties. You see, a pupil of mine was there on a scholarship. His name was Alfie, and his father sells vegetables from a barrow on the London streets. Except that he had a very good brain, everything was wrong with Alfie—wrong accent, wrong table manners, and a terrible shyness. In fact—"

He broke off. He had been about to say, "In fact, in many ways Alfie reminded me of myself when I was ten."

As the silence lengthened Judith said, "Yes?"

"There was also another boy, the only one we had whose father was a peer. This boy already had been booted out of two first-rate schools, for good and sufficient reasons, but our school, being third-rate, was happy to have an Honorable on its rolls, even if he was a nasty little sadist, which he certainly was. The Honorable Bertram took to tormenting Alfie in any way he could. Finally one day he came up behind Alfie, caught

III

him by the collar of his uniform jacket, and ripped it loose at the shoulder seams. Since his scholarship didn't include uniforms, I imagine it was a bit hard for Alfie's parents to have supplied that jacket. Anyway, he turned on his tormentor, kicked his shins and bloodied his nose, and sent him howling."

"How did you get mixed up in it?"

"A Latin master and I had seen the incident. We both went to the headmaster. The Latin teacher, who knew which side his bread was buttered on, said that Alfie's attack on Bertram had been unprovoked. The headmaster chose to believe him rather than me. Alfie was expelled. It makes me sick to think of what his parents must have felt when their kid, the kid they must have been so proud of, came dragging his small self back to them. I protested and—Well, I got the sack too."

He did not add that one form his protest had taken was punching the Latin master in his lying mouth. He said, with quiet passion, "I hate injustice." Then, feeling embarrassed by his own words, he changed the subject. "I've seen Steven Grenville around the palace quite often lately."

"Yes. He's keeping watch on preparations for the sound and light show, you know."

Kyle nodded. He wanted to ask, "Do you see him other places?" But of course that was none of his business.

He knew that he had no real reason to dislike Steven Grenville, and probably even less reason to suspect him of having caused his wife's death. After all, the police were not stupid, no matter what the popular folklore, and if they had cleared him, which evidently they had, then in all probability he was innocent. Kyle reflected that probably he disliked Grenville so much simply because every time he saw the man he was reminded of the wife who had cuckolded him, not only with Kyle himself but many others.

Of course this quiet American girl, with her not-quite-beautiful face that still was so like her beautiful cousin's, also reminded him of Cecily. But she was so unlike Cecily in every other respect that he could forget that resemblance.

Judith looked at her watch. "I had better go now. I want to get to the grocer's before he closes. Thanks very much for the drink."

Three afternoons later, as she was walking back to the car park after a sketching session in Bushey Park, she saw Kyle moving toward her. He said, "I've been looking for you. My Aunt Sara from Barnbridge Wells is visiting Mother and me. Aunt Sara is the one I stayed with while I attended the university near there. It's the first time she's ventured away from her village since she had a slight stroke last winter. Will you join the three of us for tea?"

"Tea? Why, it's almost six o'clock!"

He smiled. "This will be what in non-U circles is known as high tea. In America you would call it supper. Please come. My mother would like you to very much."

Judith doubted that. Twice lately when she had been talking with Kyle, Mrs. Hodge had approached, given Judith a wintry little smile, and summoned her son back to the apartment on the grounds that his services were needed, the first time to raise a balky window, and the second to change the globe in the kitchen ceiling light. Nevertheless, Judith decided to accept the tea invitation. Sooner or later Mrs. Hodge was going to have to face the fact that her son was twenty-six years old, and both attracted and attractive to women.

She said, "Well, if you think I look all right." Because

the day had seemed to threaten rain she had worn dark pants and an old navy blue shirt, and tied a navy blue scarf around her head.

"You look perfectly fine."

She and Kyle walked on toward the car park. Suddenly Judith halted. Ahead was a yellow van with the words "The Living Nightmares" painted in green on its side. "What on earth!"

"It's that rock group. They're posing for an album cover photo on that bridge over the moat, with the King's Beasts—you know, those gargoylish sculptures—in the background."

"The King's Beasts! On a rock album cover? They just can't! How did they ever get permission?"

"You forget that Britain is hard up. And the Nightmares bring in much-needed foreign exchange, just the way the Stones have, and before them the Beatles."

They moved on toward the palace entrance. The huge building itself was closed to visitors for the night now, with uniformed guards standing at the entrance to the first courtyard, Base Court. But the grounds were still open to the public. Thus a crowd of curious adults and excited youngsters, held back by more guards, had gathered near the bridge across the moat. Closer to the bridge a crew of men were setting up cameras and floodlamps. On the bridge itself the Nightmares lounged against the parapet that supported the leering, snarling King's Beasts.

With a nod to one of the guards, Kyle led Judith toward the bridge. Zack Reeve, in stage makeup and costume and with his guitar slung around his neck, moved in their direction. She knew that in ordinary clothes, rather than that skin-tight green satin jumpsuit, and stripped of the Medusa headdress and green face paint, Zack was so ordinary looking that no one on the underground would give him a second glance. Nevertheless, his present appearance was so grotesque that, as he drew close, she had an impulse to recoil screaming, as she had when she was eight and a "wild man" in a carnival side-show had lurched at her.

He said, "Hello, luv." His eyes, brown in his green-painted face, moved to Kyle.

"Hello, Zack," Judith said, and then added reluctantly. "Zack Reeve, Kyle Hodge."

The two men exchanged a perfunctory handshake. Then, probably because he had seen Kyle speak to the guard, Zack asked, "Are you one of the characters who works here?"

"No. I'm a character who's living here at the moment."

Zack stared. "You must be jiving. You mean you've got one of those grace-and-favor pads?"

"My mother has."

"And who is she? General Montgomery's widow?"

"She was a nannie. She worked for a cousin of the Queen Mother's."

"Outasight! I never knew they passed out grace-and-favors to nannies."

Judith's crisp voice broke a brief silence. "And I never knew they allowed rockers to use Hampton Court Palace for album photos."

Zack smiled. "Money talks, luv. The tax bite Her Majesty's government lays on us goes a long way toward keeping places like this one open for the trippers. So we not only get to use the bridge. We're going up there for more shots." Turning, he pointed to the tall Tudor chimneys, towering above the palace roof.

"Outasight," Judith said, with no expression whatsoever. She nodded, and then walked with Kyle past the lounging Nightmares on the bridge.

"It was through Cecily that I met him."

Kyle answered dryly, "I guessed that."

The guard admitted them to Base Court. As they started across it Judith saw George Sherill hurrying diagonally across their path. He stopped and gave Judith a cool greeting and Kyle an even cooler one. It occurred to her that George probably took a dim view of an ex-nannie living in a grace-and-favor apartment.

Judith said, "Isn't this after your office hours, George?"

"Of course it is! But how can I go home until that rock group leaves? They are even going up on the roof, and I'd better go up there with them. By the way, have you seen Steven Grenville?"

"Today? No."

"Well, he's in the palace or on the grounds somewhere, so if you do see him, please tell him I want to talk to him. I'll be in my office." He hurried on.

Kyle said, "I don't think he approves of your being with me."

"Do you mind that?"

"Of course not. Why should I care what that pompous little sod thinks?"

They climbed ancient stone stairs. Halfway down a long corridor, Kyle knocked at a door. Mrs. Hodge opened it, lips stretched into that pained smile. "How nice that you could come, Miss Dunne."

In the parlor Judith sat down in the armchair Mrs. Hodge indicated. What had this room been, Judith wondered, three or four centuries ago? A bedroom for one of the hundreds of guests of Henry the Eighth or some later monarch? Part of a royal nursery suite? What had the walls been like? Stone? Paneled?

Now, except for the mullioned windows, this might have been a room in almost any lower middle-class London neighborhood. Plaster walls painted a pale pink. A cheerful floral rug. Numerous small tables holding photographs. A swift glance at the two on the table beside her chair told Judith that one must be a picture of Mrs. Hodge's former employer, now a dowager duchess, and her children. She knew that the other one, showing a thin, dark boy of about six at the knee of a gentle-faced man in a suit that did not quite fit him, must be that of Kyle and his long-dead father. In the center of the room stood a round dining table, set with flat silver and four china plates.

A woman came into the room, carrying a tray which held a small ham. When the woman had placed the tray on the table, Mrs. Hodge said, "This is my sister, Sara Smeaton."

She was perhaps five years younger than Mrs. Hodge, even taller and stronger looking, and much plainer, with small gray eyes and a large nose. Judith said, "How do you do, Mrs. Smeaton?" The name seemed to stir a memory. Somewhere not too long ago she had heard that name, or read it.

"*Miss* Smeaton." The woman gave a merry smile which made her plain face surprisingly attractive. "And I don't mind in the least. In fact, I'm just grateful that our Uncle Albert realized a long time ago that Flora here would probably get a husband, and I wouldn't."

"Oh, Sara!" Kyle's mother gave a strained little laugh. "Why do you have to talk to people you've just met about —personal matters?"

"Oh, bosh, Flora, what's the harm?" Sara said, and took a Lazy Susan, laden with various condiments, from the sideboard and set it beside the ham.

Nevertheless it was not until they were halfway through tea—a very high tea indeed with cold ham, cold sliced chicken, sliced tomatoes, sweet pickles, three kinds of bread, and two kinds of cake—that Kyle's aunt returned to the topic of Uncle Albert. He had emigrated to Australia and made money—"not a lot, but some"—in sheep ranching. "He came home for the last time when I was eighteen and Flora was twenty-two. A very frank man, Uncle Albert was. He told me he thought I was going to really need his money and so he was going to leave it to me. And that's what he did. Oh, not that his money turned me into a lady of leisure. I'm a sister—what you in the states call a nurse—and I've worked in lots of hospitals, including the biggest ones in London. But thanks to Uncle Albert I was always able to quit whenever Flora needed to leave Kyle with me."

"Really, Sara!"

"Oh, come off it, Flora. There was no disgrace in your becoming a widow, and needing help now and then. And certainly things have finally worked out well for you as well as me. Imagine the duchess pulling strings so you could get in here—"

"Sara! How can you use such expressions?"

Sara looked puzzled, then amused. "Oh, I see. A duchess doesn't pull strings. She uses her influence. But anyway, as I've often said to Kyle, it is strange and wonderful that you should be living here, when there's that old story in our family—"

"Sara!" Now Mrs. Hodge looked definitely angry. A fleeting glance at Kyle told Judith that he too was feeling uncomfortable, although she could not tell whether it was because of the nature of the "old story" or just the clash between the two women.

Hoping to create a diversion Judith said, "You are certainly right about this being a wonderful place to live. Whenever I get to thinking that I know the palace and the grounds thoroughly I discover some marvelous bit of wall carving I'd never noticed before, or some little pond over in Bushey Park."

Kyle said, "I keep discovering new things too." His smile thanked her for changing the subject. "But that's nothing to wonder at, when you consider that for four-and-a-half centuries the royal tenants have been adding embellishments to the palace and grounds."

Mrs. Hodge said, "Like the pictures of all those hussies of his that Charles the Second had someone paint."

"Lely," her son said.

"Well, whoever the painter was, I sometimes wonder why a respectable royal family like the one we have now allows those pictures to hang there for everyone to gawk at."

The conversation became easier after that. But still the "old story" Mrs. Hodge had not wanted her sister to tell seemed to hang in the air, bringing a certain constraint to everyone's manner. As soon as she felt she could do so without giving offense, Judith expressed her thanks, tied the head scarf beneath her chin, and said goodbye. When she descended to Base Court she saw that although the sky was very dark, rain had not yet begun to fall. She hurried toward the gate.

A watcher, looking down from the height, for a moment saw a young woman in a dark gown and wimple, crossing the ancient brick pavement. Then the illusion passed, and she was once more just a girl in pants and a shirt and head scarf, hurrying toward the gate.

12

She saw no Nightmares on the bridge. Evidently they had not left the premises, though, because their yellow van still stood in the car park. She had just gotten into her own car when the first drops of rain struck the roof. By the time she emerged from the palace grounds the rain was pouring down, and it increased in volume as she drove down the narrow road to The Columns. She found the wrought-iron gates standing open. With all those able-bodied men on the premises, neither she nor the Children of Emmanuel saw any need to keep the gates locked. As she drove back to her apartment, she heard voices singing "Shall We Gather at the River?" and realized that it was Wednesday, prayer meeting night.

She was unlocking her door when she heard the telphone's ring. She hurried inside, flipped on the hall light and the living room light, and lifted the phone from its cradle.

"Hello, Judith," Steven Grenville said. "I thought you'd be home about now. I saw you leaving the palace."

"You did? I didn't see you."

"I was on the top floor of Base Court. They're rigging lights up there for the *son et lumière.*" He paused. "George Sherill said he'd seen you earlier with Kyle Hodge."

"Yes. I had tea, I mean high tea, with him and his mother and his aunt."

"I see." After several seconds he added, "Will you have dinner with me tomorrow night?"

His voice, rapid and almost harsh, gave the impression of a man speaking against his own will. Judith could understand his conflict all too well, because it was similar to her own. He found himself attracted to a girl whose face was a haunting reminder of his dead wife. She found herself attracted to a man who admittedly had hated her cousin, who on at least one occasion had struck her, and who might just possibly have killed her.

Steven said, "Well?"

She heard herself say, in the stilted voice of a fifteen-year-old who has just been asked to the junior prom, "Why, I'd like that very much."

They drove in to London and had dinner the next evening at a restaurant in Knightsbridge. Later they went to a newly opened night spot in Sloane Square where a small rhythm-and-blues band played for dancing. Somehow through most of the evening Judith and Steven managed to keep the conversation on such safe topics as the coming sound and light show at Hampton Court Palace and the tennis matches at Wimbledon. But on the way home an uneasy silence settled between them. Judith wondered if he would expect to be asked into her apartment. And if so, what would she do about it?

Barney had never asked her for a pledge of fidelity, nor had she given one. Nevertheless, she had been faithful until now. What was more, she had felt no temptation not to be. And there of course was another and perhaps stronger reason why she should keep Steven out of her apartment. She looked at him from the corner of her eyes, this widower of her cousin. In the upward-striking light from the dashboard his face with its distinct planes of cheekbones and jaw looked closed, unreadable.

He drove through the open gates of The Columns, went past the darkened house, and stopped at the foot of the carriage-house steps. The two of them climbed to the landing. "Let me," Steven said, and took the key from her hand.

He unlocked the door, pushed it open. He looked down at her, his face a pale blur in the darkness. She said, again aware of how stilted she sounded, "Thank you for a lovely evening."

He went on looking down at her, while the pulse in the hollow of her throat stepped up its beat. Then he said, "Goodnight, Judith."

Half relieved, half chagrined, she watched his dark figure partway down the stairs, and then went inside and closed the door.

During the three weeks that followed Judith not only caught frequent glimpses of Steven at the palace. She went out with him several times too. On each occasion he left her at her door with an abrupt goodnight. Judith wondered if he behaved with equal restraint when he dated other girls.

She knew that he did date them. One evening as she drove home from the palace she saw him and an extremely attractive red-haired girl emerge from the pub where she herself had had drinks with Kyle on two occasions. One night in London, as she sat alone in an inexpensive gallery seat in a Shaftsbury Avenue theater, she had looked down and seen Steven and the same redhead in fifth row center seats.

She herself went out with Kyle Hodge several times, even though she knew that the result would be an even more wintry smile from his mother the next time they encountered each other on the Hampton Court grounds or in the palace itself. Because she suspected that Kyle had little money to spend, Judith suggested inexpensive pleasures, such as a ride on the Thames steamer as far as Greenwich. Twice they drove into London in Kyle's second-hand Morris for dinner at a Chinese restaurant and a movie afterward. Handsome as Kyle was, she did not find him as physically attractive as Steven. But partly for that reason her dates with Kyle were more pleasant, not more exciting but more pleasant. It was enjoyable indeed to sit with this intelligent and sensitive young man in some inexpensive restaurant, or on the top deck of a steamer with the willow-studded shore slipping past, and talk of almost everything, from politics to poetry and ESP to ecology.

On an evening in late July, Steven Grenville took her to Chadwell's, a London restaurant and gambling club where their dinner alone must have cost as much as several evenings she had spent with Kyle. As they were having coffee Steven asked her if she would like to try a few turns at the roulette or blackjack tables.

Judith shook her head. "Perhaps it's because I'm of Scots descent on my mother's side, but gambling doesn't attract me. Even if I won, the thought that I might have lost would take all the fun out of it."

He smiled slightly. She could almost hear him thinking that Scottish blood on the maternal side had not kept Cecily from gambling. He said, "Then let's have a brandy in the bar."

They moved from the main dining room into a smaller room set with leather-upholstered banquettes. On a raised platform two comedians, with no facial expression whatsoever, discussed the royal family in irreverent and hilarious terms.

The comedians had just bowed to enthusiastic applause when a short, thin man started past Steven and Judith's table and then halted. "Why, Grenville! Good to see you."

There were no scars on his sharp-featured face, and no diamond rings on the hand he thrust toward Steven. His dark pin-striped suit, far from looking like a gangster's, might have belonged to a member of any club along Pall Mall. And yet instantly Judith sensed that the man was not only corrupt but dangerous.

Reluctantly Steven got to his feet, and even more reluctantly clasped the extended hand. "Hello, Tolliver." Then, as the stranger's gaze moved to Judith's face and rested there, "Miss Dunne, Mr. Tolliver."

"I'm pleased to know you, Miss Dunne." He looked at Steven. "Mind if I join you and the young lady?"

"Sorry. We were just about to ask for the check."

After a moment Tolliver smiled and said softly, "Now is that any way to treat a chap you've done business with?"

Steven's high-cheekboned face flushed and then paled. Tolliver laughed. "Not to worry, old boy. One thing everyone knows about me. Once I've made a deal to keep my lip buttoned, I keep it buttoned. Well, I think I'll try my luck at the crap table."

As Tolliver moved toward an archway in the far wall, Steven sat down again. Judith felt her stomach knotting up. What sort of deal had Steven made with that ferret-faced man? She had a vision of the two of them in a rear booth of some pub, or more likely in a car parked on a lonely road. "You'll have to get it all done by eleven-thirty, because those architectural dinners never last much later than that."

Steven said in a low, constrained voice, "I suppose I'd better tell you what he meant. About six months after we were married Cecily and a few of her friends smuggled in some cocaine from Turkey and sold it. She didn't need the money, of course. It was the kicks she was after. Anyway, Tolliver heard of it—in fact, one of Cecily's friends was a friend of his—and he saw a way of cashing in. He came to me and said that unless I paid him two thousand pounds he'd tell the police about Cecily's smuggling."

Judith forced words through her tight throat. "Why didn't he go straight to Cecily?"

"I don't know. Perhaps because he felt she would be reckless enough to defy him, and count upon expensive lawyers to get the charge against her dismissed. I, on the other hand, felt that if I wanted to keep my wife out of prison, I had better pay up."

She said, wanting to believe him and yet not quite able to, "But they say that once you pay blackmail you'll probably have to pay it again. Weren't you afraid he'd come back?"

"If he had, I'd have told him to go ahead and tell the police. I think he knew that. He knew that two thousand pounds was all he could get out of me. As in any other sort of enterprise, a man to be successful at blackmail has to be able to judge how much the traffic will bear." He fell silent for a moment and then said in a flat, cold voice, "You don't believe me, do you?"

She just looked at him, unable to speak.

"Shall I tell you what you do believe, or almost believe? You think that a few minutes ago the man I hired to kill Cecily was standing close enough to you to touch you." When she still didn't speak he added, "Well?"

At last she managed to say, "You yourself told me that some people think—" She broke off and then added swiftly, "It's not that I want to believe anything like that!"

"But you can't help thinking it might be true. Well, I

suppose that's to be expected." He paused and then asked abruptly, "Shall I take you home now?"

They drove to Hampton Court in almost complete silence. Judith huddled wretchedly in her corner of the seat. She felt pity for this man who, in all probability innocent, might for the rest of his days be suspected of hiring someone to murder his wife. And she felt sorry for herself, too. It was unlikely indeed, after tonight, that this man to whom she felt such a powerful attraction would ask her out again. And even if he did, she did not know whether, after tonight, she could subdue her distrust sufficiently to want to see him again.

Suddenly another thought tightened her nerves. If he *were* guilty, wouldn't he be wondering now what she intended to do? For all he knew, she might go to the police, describe tonight's meeting between Steven and Tolliver, and suggest that they find out what the little man was doing the night of Cecily's death.

She would never do that. She would not cause the police to grill Steven again, not when she felt that there was only a small chance of his guilt. She wanted to turn to him and tell him that, but embarrassment held her back. And fear. Best not to plant in his mind even the possibility that she might go to the police. Because after all there was that small chance that the man sitting beside her *was* a murderer by proxy. And if he decided that she might prove dangerous to him—

He turned in at The Columns' gates, drove through the darkness back to the carriage house. There was nothing to be afraid of, she told herself, at least not at this moment. There were sixteen adults and children in that house only a few yards away.

Steven reached across her and unlatched the door. He said, in that flat, cold voice, "I'm sure you won't mind my not climbing the stairs with you."

"No, of course not."

She got out. Before she reached the foot of the stairs he was already backing the car swiftly toward the gate. She hurried up the stairs, went into her apartment, and locked the door.

13

FOR THE NEXT two days her work did not go at all well. On both days she sat until seven o'clock, an hour after the last visitor had left the palace, in the small Banqueting House—a kind of eighteenth-century playroom with nude gods and goddesses frolicking over walls and ceilings—which William the Third had built down by the river. Again and again she tried to draw long-nosed William and his friends feasting at a table laden with the boiled beef, roast mutton, roast goose, quails, capons, and venison which were served at royal meals in those days. But the drawing simply would not come right. The human figures seated around the table seemed to have no more animation than the roast goose resting upon it.

On the second evening, sketching case in hand, she wandered back through the palace grounds to the avenues of yew trees beyond the building's east front. She sat down on a bench beneath one of the pyramid-shaped trees. She had no doubt of why she couldn't work. Her mind was too filled with thoughts of a man named Tolliver, and of Steven, and his abrupt leave-taking of her the night before last.

The light had begun to fade. Guards politely told visitors strolling about the grounds that they must leave. Because they knew that Judith had special privileges, none of them approached her. At last, with a start, she looked at her watch. Almost nine-thirty.

She rose and walked back to the palace. The guard on duty at the east front entrance let her through. Footsteps echoing in the silence, she walked back through Fountain Court. If attendants were supposed to turn off the fountain at night, they as yet had not done so. The plume of water, pale in the fading twilight, still rose from the circular basin. She moved down a stone-floored corridor to the open space called Clock Court, because of the huge, brightly painted clock above one of its archways, and then along another corridor to Base Court. Here lights from windows of the grace-and-favor apartments relieved the gloom somewhat. Nevertheless, it was dark enough that she did not want to cut across the brick pavement, worn to unevenness by the centuries, to the entrance. Instead she moved along the walk close to the courtyard's northern wall.

Afterward she could never be sure whether or not she heard the stone missile before it struck. Perhaps there had been a faint, grating sound as it parted from the coping. Perhaps air disturbed by its plunge registered against her eardrums as a sighing noise. All she was sure of was the explosive sound behind her as it struck the walk.

She whirled. Pale fragments of stone lay on the walk and on the grassy strip beside it. Her nostrils caught the acrid smell of ancient mortar, fragmented to powder by the force of the impact, Obviously a section of white capstone from the crenelated battlement had come down. She stood motionless, paralyzed by the realization that it had missed her by only three or four feet.

Men were moving toward her now. Two guards from the palace's west entrance. Another guard from Clock

Court. He said, "Are you all right, Miss Dunne?" Even in that dim light she could see the frightened look on his elderly face.

"I think so."

In the courtyard's northern wall windows were going up. Voices called down to ask what the trouble was.

"It's all right," the guard called back. "Some masonry fell, but no one was hurt."

One of the two other guards, a younger man, pointed up to the roof. "It came from up there. Even in this light you can see where a capstone is missing."

"Wait till Mr. Sherill hears of this," the old man said ominously. "Why do we have masons and bricklayers here and even an architect, except to keep the old place in good repair? Oh, Mr. Sherill won't be half mad, he won't."

The third guard asked, "You're sure none of that hit you, miss?"

"I'm sure."

"All the same, we'd best see you to your car."

Shaken by the thought that if the stone had struck her she would be lying dead now, Judith was glad of the guards' company out to the car park. She got into the Volvo, thanked the men, and drove out of the palace grounds. It was not until she turned onto the road that she became aware of a damp stickiness on her right leg a little below the knee. She pulled over to the side of the road and stopped.

Already the leg of her green cotton pants was stuck to the wound. Wincing, she pulled the cloth free and rolled the pants leg above her knee. As nearly as she could tell, the cut from which the blood oozed was at least two inches long. But in her shock at the thought of what a direct hit by that chunk of stone would have done to her, she had not even felt a fragment of it strike her leg.

She remembered that on the Hampton Court Village high street, which just ahead curved away from the road, there was a small house with a sign attached to its low stone fence: "Samuel Birdsley, M.D." Judith took several paper tissues from her shoulder bag, plastered them to the wound, rolled down her pants leg, and drove to the doctor's fake Tudor cottage. As she went up its walk she saw that a sign, "Doctor's Office," beside the main doorway pointed toward another door in a one-story wing of the house. The windows of the wing were dark, but Judith rang the bell anyway.

A light went on inside. A moment later the door opened and a white-haired man who looked rather like a diminutive Thomas A. Edison peered out at her. "Yes?"

"Dr. Birdsley?"

"I am."

"I have a cut on my leg. I'm afraid it's bleeding."

"Don't worry on our account. That's why we have linoleum on the floors in this part of the house. Come on in."

In the small surgery he rolled up her pants leg, gently pulled the paper tissues away, and looked at the welling wound. As he bathed it he asked, "How did this happen?"

She told him.

"Strange," he said. "The Department of the Environment tries to keep all the places like Hampton Court Palace free of hazards to visitors. It has to. Otherwise the government would be paying out thousands of pounds in damages each year. Strange that a loose section of stone should have been overlooked."

Ever since the first shock had worn off, Judith had been thinking the same thing.

"Well, this cut isn't bad," Dr. Birdsley said. "Stitches

won't be necessary. You'll have a scar for a while, but not permanently."

He sterilized the cut and bandaged it. After thanking him, Judith walked out to her car. As she drove down the tree-bordered road toward The Columns, she found herself unable to stop picturing a dark figure up there on the palace roof. Someone who knew that section of capstone was loose, or even someone who himself had loosened it. Someone who knew that she often stayed late at the palace, and who, tonight, might have observed her sitting on the bench under the yew tree as the day faded into twilight.

It could have been Kyle up there on the palace roof. The capstone had hurtled down from a point above and only a few feet to the right of his mother's living room windows. But it was hard to believe that he would have any reason to want her dead. Now his mother might want that, she reflected, with a faint, grim smile, but it was hard to imagine a woman, even one as sturdy as Mrs. Hodge, pushing a heavy capstone down into the courtyard.

As for George Sherill, he obviously disliked her. If he had gained an inkling that she knew of his affair with Cecily, he probably more than disliked her. And if he was the one who had written that threatening letter to Cecily, and if he had any idea that Judith might have found it and turned it over to the police, he must both hate and fear her. True, George's usual day in his office ended at five o'clock. But he was perfectly free to remain later at the palace, and often did.

So did Steven Grenville.

She turned in at the gates. Evidently all of the Children of Emmanuel had gone to bed, for no lights showed in the main house. She parked her car at the foot of the carriage-house stairs. On the landing she unlocked the door, switched on the light, stepped inside. She hesitated in the hallway, reminding herself again that it was most unlikely that anyone would enter this apartment in her absence to lie in wait for her, not when there were people only a few yards away to hear her scream. Nevertheless, even before laying down her shoulder bag, she opened the drawer of that stand beside her bed. The gun was there, and its clip was still full.

She walked back into the living room and stood indecisively in its center for a moment. Then, feeling weighted with reluctance, she walked over to the phone and dialed Steven's number. The phone at the other end of the line rang again and again. After awhile she hung up.

He strode along the nighttime London street, so rapidly and with such a confident, even triumphant, smile on his face that passersby looked at him curiously. Caught up in his own euphoria, he paid other pedestrians little notice. Nevertheless he was aware that, as sometimes happened, people from the past mingled with the present-day Londoners in their jeans from King's Road and their sweaters and skirts from Mark and Spencer and their quietly expensive clothes from Bond Street. Now and then he caught a glimpse of a rich merchant in a fur-trimmed cloak, or an apprentice in breeches and hose, or a long-gowned figure whose flat velvet cap marked him as a man of the law or medicine. As always when such figures appeared to him, he welcomed the sight of them. It was good to feel that he moved with unassailable power through not just one century but several.

He reached a curb. A company of the king's mounted soldiers was approaching along the street, although for some reason he could not hear the horses' hooves strike the cobblestones. The riders, in short scarlet cloaks and plumed hats, swept past. He started to cross the street.

A blaring noise made his whole body tighten with shock. A voice bawled, "Mind your step, guv'nor!"

He jumped back onto the curb. The cab, its driver scowling at him, was the first of the long line of cars that moved past him. He waited, aware now that he had just emerged from one of the narrow Soho streets that ran into Oxford Street.

When the signal changed he moved, cold sweat rolling down his sides, with a number of other pedestrians to the opposite curb. He turned right, hurried past a number of closed shops, and then entered a Wimpy Bar. There amid the fluorescent glare, and with the late Jimi Hendrix's voice wailing from a loudspeaker, and the smell of frying meat heavy in the air, he sat on a stool and stared at his image in the mirror behind the counter.

In God's name what was wrong with him?

He remembered the day with complete clarity up until about five in the afternoon. After that there was a blank period. Sometime during that period he must have driven into London because, after dark, he suddenly found himself driving down Victoria Street. Too shaken to stay behind the wheel, he had left his car in a car park near Victoria Station and set out for a walk, desperately hoping to recapture his memory of the past few hours. Instead the blankness must have descended again. Obviously he had wandered on foot at least two miles—doing what, thinking what, God only knew—until the cab driver's alarmed yell had brought him out of it.

Images like a tiny fragment of some otherwise forgotten dream flashed before his mind's eye. Mounted men in scarlet coats and breeches. Had he, during that blank period, gone into a cinema that was showing a costume film? Perhaps that was it. Or perhaps the mounted men had been a hallucination.

But if so it had at least been a pleasant one, not like some of the brief flashes of nightmarish scenes he had recalled from otherwise blank stretches in his life these past few years.

And thank God he could remember this time where he had left his car. One night months earlier he had come to in the tough Cable Street district near the London docks, with no idea of where he had left his car, and no memory of anything that had happened since he had first set out, after dinner, to meet a former colleague of his in a pub near Westminster Abbey. He had walked on past shadowy tenements and decaying warehouses, sick with the knowledge that his best hope of recovering his car was to go to the police, even though he cringed inwardly at the thought of trying to answer their questions. And then suddenly he had seen his car parked at the curb a few feet ahead of him—miraculously unstolen even though he had left its key in the ignition.

"Wimpy or sausage roll?"

He jumped. "What?" The girl who stood behind the counter, in orange pants and cap and a yellow tee-shirt with Popeye's picture printed on it, looked Asiatic—Indo-Chinese or perhaps Filipino. All the people in service jobs in London these days seemed Asiatic, or Indian, or Yugoslavian, or anything but English.

Whatever her origin, she had mastered London invective. "Mister, h'all we 'ave is Wimpies and sausage rolls. If you don't want one or the other, why the bleedin' 'ell are you in 'ere?"

He hated both hamburger and sausage. "I'll have a sausage roll," he said.

14

EVIDENTLY HER narrow escape from that plunging missile had been even more of a shock than Judith had realized, so much so that as she whirled around there on the walk all her muscles must have tightened up. She awoke the next morning, after a night of broken sleep, to find herself filled with muscular aches, as if she had played several sets of tennis the day before after weeks of sedentary living.

It was nine before she summoned up the will to get out of bed, and even then she felt no desire to go to the palace, despite the fact that she knew she should make another attempt at that Banqueting House sketch. She felt not only frightened but depressed. In all probability nothing more sinister than gravity had caused that capstone to fall. And yet she had been unable to blot out the thought of Steven, who must know every foot of Hampton Court Palace, up there on the roof in the darkness—

As she stood at the window a little before ten o'clock, sipping her second cup of tea and gazing dispiritedly at the now-neat lawn between her apartment and the main house, the telephone rang. Heartbeats rapid, she was sure even before she lifted the receiver that the caller was Steven.

His voice was cool and formal. "I hear you had a near-accident last night. Do you feel any ill effects this morning?"

"Nothing serious. I discovered after I left the palace that a fragment of stone had cut my leg, but Dr. Birdsley on the village high street treated it. It's scarcely sore at all this morning."

"I see." He paused and then went on, "I've already inspected the spot from which the capstone fell. Apparently without anyone's noticing it, the mortar holding the stone to the brick had crumbled away."

She said nothing. After a moment he continued, with a certain cold defensiveness in his voice, "I realize that the mortar should have been renewed. But the palace is an enormous structure, and because of cuts in the budget the maintenance staff is much smaller than it used to be. No wonder needed repairs are sometimes overlooked."

Even though she knew the question might anger him, she had to ask it. "Did you see any sign that the stone had been loosened deliberately?"

Again he was silent for several seconds. When he finally spoke his tone was more distant than ever. "You mean chisel marks, that sort of thing? I did not, nor did any of the three masons who were with me up on the palace roof this morning."

Just the same, she reflected, the absence of chisel marks did not mean that the fall of that stone had been accidental. At almost any time in the recent past, someone might have noticed that the mortar had crumbled away. Last night he might have waited up there, sure that in the near-darkness she would keep to the walk rather than cross the uneven bricks in the court's center.

She said, "Even if there aren't any chisel marks, couldn't someone have pushed that stone over?"

"Now why should anyone have wanted to tip a hundred pounds of Portland stone over into the courtyard?" When she didn't answer, he went on, "If your imagination has led you to wonder where I was when it fell, I was a good twenty miles away, at a party in St. John's Wood."

And, she added silently, no doubt with plenty of witnesses, just as he'd had plenty of witnesses to his presence in the London the night Cecily was killed. She said, "Well, thanks for calling to see how I am."

She expected him to say goodbye then. Instead he said, after a moment, "I shall be away today and tomorrow. I'm needed at the Brighton Pavillion."

"You're leaving, even though the sound and light show is coming up?"

"I've done all that is necessary for the show. Besides, it isn't until Friday. I'll be back by then, in case you want to get in touch with me about that falling capstone or anything else. Goodbye," he said abruptly, and hung up.

By two in the afternoon she decided that, rather than wander aimlessly around the apartment, she would take another stab at the Banqueting House sketch. When she reached the palace she saw that the grandstand seats for the sound and light show already had been placed on the wide lawn facing the moat bridge and the entrance to Base Court.

By six she felt that her drawing, although not apt to win any awards, would get by. Unwilling to return to her too-silent apartment, she strolled through the dwindling number of visitors over to Bushey Park. She moved past the Diana Fountain, where as always a few children leaned over the coping around the shallow circular pool, and then moved down a path that led into the wilder part of the park, where the grass and the spreading branches of oaks and maples had been allowed to grow almost as unchecked as they would have in a true wilderness. She stopped finally in a secluded little dell, set up her easel, and began to draw a lily-covered pond and the small footbridge that arched above it. She was making the sketch, not because it was needed for Barney's book, but for the distraction it offered her. Soon she was so absorbed in her work that she was only dimly aware of the distant voices of people who occasionally moved along some path. She was conscious, though, of the changing color of the light. She wielded her charcoal more rapidly, hoping to finish the sketch before sunset glow, slanting through the trees to gleam on the water and dye the white pond lilies pink, changed the whole mood of the scene before her.

"Hello there."

She whirled around. Because the sunset light was behind him, it took her a moment to identify the tall, slender man who stood about fifteen feet away on the path. "Oh, Kyle! You startled me."

"Sorry. I didn't want to. That is why I stopped back here." He moved toward her. "One of the guards told me he'd seen you walking toward Bushey, so I came looking for you. I've been wondering how you are. I mean, I heard about that capstone almost hitting you last night."

"I'm fine, except for a small cut on my leg. You weren't here yesterday evening?"

"No, I drove into London." His voice suddenly sounded constrained. "I'm awfully glad you weren't hurt. And since you weren't, will you have dinner with me tonight?"

"Kyle, I'm sorry. But even though I'm physically okay, I still feel too—shaky to be good company. Could we make it tomorrow night instead?"

"I wish we could. But I've already told my Aunt Sara over the phone that I'll go up to Barnbridge Wells tomorrow and spend the night at her place. You see, day after tomorrow is her birthday. Mother doesn't feel up to going, and so I think I'd better. After all, she did have a stroke not too long ago. And although she doesn't complain about it, I'm sure that these days she feels depressed and uneasy about living alone."

"I understand. Incidentally, I liked Miss Smeaton very much."

He nodded. "I spent a lot of my childhood with her, and of course I lived with her while I was going to the university near Barnbridge Wells. She's not an educated woman in the formal sense, but she's intelligent. And she has read a lot, especially history. I've always found her a stimulating person."

Although he didn't say so, Judith gathered that he found his aunt better company than his mother. Suddenly she exclaimed, "Now I know where I'd heard the name Smeaton! What reminded me was your saying that your aunt liked history. I remember from the first Hampton Court book by my friend back in New York that a Michael Smeaton had something to do with Anne Boleyn's treason trial. Is that right?"

After a moment he said, "You're wrong about the name. It was Mark Smeaton. But you're right about the rest of it."

"Was he an ancestor of yours?"

"He was, or at least according to the story Aunt Sara first told me when I was about twelve years old. Mark was not a gentleman, you know." Kyle's voice had taken on a strange coldness. "In fact, the records of Anne Boleyn's trial show that other witnesses referred to him contemptuously as a plowboy. But he had musical talent. He could not only play the lute and sing, but compose songs too. And so a place was found for him at Hampton Court Palace."

He stopped speaking for a moment. When he resumed,

his voice was even colder. "He had a sweetheart in his village, a girl of his own class. The story is that she discovered after he left that she was pregnant. Maybe he never knew about it. Maybe she did get a message to him at Hampton Court and he did—or did not—send back words that he would marry her. Anyway, after his death she went to a village some distance from her own, where she called herself Mistress Smeaton, and gave birth to a son."

"And he's the Smeaton you are descended from?"

"According to the story in the family, yes."

She was remembering more about Mark Smeaton now. "He was executed, wasn't he?"

"Yes. After Henry the Eighth decided to get rid of Anne, Mark Smeaton and four other men, including her own brother, were beheaded on the charge that they had committed adultery with her." His voice had thickened. "But they distinguished plowboy Mark from the gentlemen, of course. The courtiers were merely killed. Mark was tortured first, tortured until he was ready to say anything King Henry wanted him to. He not only confessed that he had been to bed with the queen. At his interrogator's insistence, he named the four other men, including Anne's brother."

Judith felt frightened by something in his voice, and in the flush that made his olive-skinned face even darker. And yet a strange fascination caused her to continue the conversation. "Then you think Mark Smeaton was innocent?"

"Of making love to the queen? Probably not. But if they were lovers, you can be sure it was Anne who did the seducing. No plowboy would have dared to make even the faintest of overtures to a queen. But Anne had a strong motive for taking a healthy young man to bed. She knew her only hope of holding onto Henry and maybe even onto her head was to bear a male heir to the throne. And Henry, who was probably syphilitic by that time, didn't seem likely to spawn anything but miscarriages or children too weak to survive more than a few years."

His voice gathered speed. "Yes, I think she took him to bed all right, that plowboy turned musician. Dazzled as he must have been by her, she found it easy to use him. And because she had used him, the poor country oaf found himself first in the torture chamber, and then kneeling with his head on the block."

"But Kyle, Anne went to the block too."

"So she did. But she'd always known that might happen. From the moment she met Henry she'd been playing for high stakes—to get him to divorce his first wife, and to be crowned queen herself, and to hang onto her crown after she got it. Mark, on the other hand, was just a village clod who probably really thought the queen loved him. As I see it, she more or less deserved what happened to her. Mark didn't."

Judith thought, as she looked at the dark, bitter face, it's almost as if he had been there in those days. No, it was more than that. It was almost as if he himself—

She said swiftly, "Kyle, I'm sure that it was a great injustice. But there have always been injustices."

His face swung toward her. For a moment he just looked at her through the deepening twilight. Then he smiled. It was a smile that held no merriment whatever, only a cold, dangerous hatred. With a leap of terror she knew that it was no longer Kyle standing there. The person who looked out at her from his dark eyes was someone she had never met.

He said, "Injustice, lady? What would someone like you know about injustice?"

Lady. Heart hammering in her throat she thought,

who is it that he thinks I am?

Aware of their isolation and the growing dark, she tried to banish that stranger she saw looking out of his eyes. "Kyle, about that dinner date—"

He took a step toward her. "It was because of you that wisteria vine was cut down, wasn't it? It happened after you got here, so you must have gone to Grenville about the vine, and he ordered it cut."

She whispered, "Please, please—"

Then, giddy with relief, she heard the voices of approaching people. A man and two women emerged from a path on the opposite side of the lily pond and moved toward the bridge. Swiftly, determined that they would not leave her behind with this man who stood close enough to touch her now, Judith turned to her drawing board. She removed the thumbtacks that held the sketch, tearing the paper slightly in her haste.

Kyle said, in a completely normal tone, "Let me help you." He opened the case, took the sketch from her hand and placed it inside, and then began to fold the easel.

The man and two women had crossed the bridge now. In another second or so they would have left the dell. Turning to them Judith said, with the bright edge of hysteria in her voice, "This is a lovely spot, isn't it?"

The trio halted. Perhaps, like many English, they found it startling to be addressed by a stranger. Perhaps they sensed something odd in the atmosphere. Whatever the reason, there was a brief silence. Then one of the women said, "Quite lovely."

At least she had caused them to halt for the necessary few moments. Her sketching case was packed now. She stretched out her hand for it. Kyle said, "I'll carry this to your car for you."

Already the three strangers were several yards away up the path. "All right, but I want to hurry. I must get back to my apartment. I'm—I'm expecting a phone call from my parents."

He smiled. "Then we'll hurry."

They set out at a brisk pace which soon carried them past the man and his two companions. But no matter. They were on a much wider path by then, filled with people who, now that it was almost closing time, moved toward the car park or toward the exit gate near the bus stop. Now Kyle was talking about some engine trouble with his car. Because of it, he would have to take a morning train into Waterloo Station and from there take another train to his aunt's village.

They had reached the car park. He opened her car door for her and then, when she was behind the wheel, handed her her drawing case. As she switched on the ignition he stepped back from the car and said, smiling, "Goodnight, Judith."

So she was Judith to him now. But there in the darkening woodland, when he had addressed her as "lady," who had he believed her to be? Herself? Cecily? Or a young woman who had died on Tower Green one May morning four and a half centuries ago?

As she drove out of the palace grounds and through the village, the first lines of that grotesque jingle kept going through her head:

> Annie and Cee-cee and Miss Judith Dunne
> Think they are three but to me are all one.

She had assumed that the Annie of the jingle was Annette Swayle, part-time servant girl to the Grenvilles. But now she felt almost certain that Annie was Anne Boleyn, that woman who might have, in Kyle's bitter phrase, "used" an ignorant youth from the country, and thus brought about his torture and death.

And Kyle. Who was he? Not just the sensitive, intelligent young man she knew and liked, but someone else also. Someone who had looked out at her from Kyle's eyes only minutes ago.

What sort of things did that other person do when he was in control? Invade an empty house to fondle by candlelight a cleaver which had taken a young woman's life? Climb an outside staircase to slip a jingle of his own composition under the door of another young woman?

That hideous thing he must have done last August she could not bring herself to think about, not here on this lonely road with her headlights tunneling through the darkness.

She turned in at the gates. Unwilling tonight to leave them standing open as usual, she got out and locked the gates behind her. After all, the Children of Emmanuel had their own key. She drove down the driveway. Lights shone from the downstairs front windows of the main house, and, in the rear, from upstairs windows, illuminating the back lawn and the stairs up to her apartment. Quickly she climbed to her door and unlocked it. After turning on the hall light she relocked the back door and shot the bolt home.

In the living room she closed the draperies and then sank onto the sofa. She'd had nothing to eat since, around five that afternoon, she had bought tea and an apple tart at the palace's outdoor restaurant. And yet she had no desire to prepare dinner, not with that jingle running through her head.

According to the rhymester, she herself, and her dead cousin, and "Annie" were all the same. She realized now that between herself and her cousin on the one hand, and certain portraits of King Henry's dark-eyed, dark-haired second wife on the other, there was a fairly strong resemblance.

She forced herself to consider the last two lines:

I keep a count as Death scythes down the row:
Two of them down and one left to go.

Two of them dead, one on Tower Green centuries ago, and one less than a year ago in that room a few yards away. And to that other self she had seen looking from Kyle's eyes they were both the same—the woman who had dazzled his plowboy ancestor, and beautiful Cecily Grenville, who must in some way have both dazzled and outraged Kyle himself.

But why, she wondered numbly, was her own name in that jingle? She had done him no harm. What did she have in common with Cecily and long-dead Anne except facial resemblance? But perhaps, in the logic of that other Kyle, that was enough.

What should she do? Go to the police again? What could she offer as evidence—her own opinion that he had "behaved strangely" beside a lily pond in Bushey Park?

And anyway, even if she had had real evidence to take to the police, she would not have wanted to bring about his arrest in that way. Oh, if what she suspected was true then certainly he had to be locked up. But she had always liked and respected him. What was more, the Kyle she knew probably had no knowledge of that jingle, or the cleaver hidden in a fireplace in an empty house, or—again her mind shied away—of what that other self might have done earlier. For those reasons, she wanted him to be treated as gently as possible.

Steven. She would consult Steven. She dialed his number. It was only after his phone had rung half a dozen times that she remembered him telling her that he was going to Brighton.

She hung up, went into her bedroom, and again made sure that the gun was still in the nightstand drawer, and still loaded. Then she sat down in an armchair beside the bed. She knew she would not sleep tonight, not when the stranger she had talked to beside the lily pond might be prowling through the dark. And so instead she would sit here and try to decide what to do about Kyle Hodge.

15

Toward morning she did fall asleep. When she came confusedly awake in the armchair, with the lamp beside her still turned on and daylight showing through a crack in the draperies, she looked at her watch. A quarter of eleven.

Kyle had said he would take a morning train from Waterloo Station today. Surely then, he must long since have left Hampton Court Palace. And so she would do what in the early morning hours she had decided was best. She would go to see Kyle's mother.

Almost an hour later she skirted the northern edge of Base Court, passed the spot where the plunging capstone had shattered to bits, and turned under an ancient archway. She climbed the worn stairs and knocked on Mrs. Hodge's door.

Judith heard footsteps inside. A split second after Mrs. Hodge opened the door, her polite welcoming smile began to fade. Judith said, "Forgive me for disturbing you, Mrs. Hodge."

The older woman's reply was indirect. "My son isn't here."

"I know." She had made sure of that before she even drove onto the palace grounds. The guard at the gate had told her, in answer to her question, that he had seen Mrs. Hodge and her son walking toward the railway station around ten-thirty that morning. Around eleven Mrs. Hodge had returned, alone.

"You're the one I want to see," Judith said. "It's very important."

With obvious reluctance Mrs. Hodge opened the door wider. "Come in." When Judith had stepped past her she added, "Please sit down."

With Judith in an overstuffed armchair, and Mrs. Hodge on the overstuffed sofa, they faced each other in that fussy but neat parlor. Mrs. Hodge said, "What is it, Miss Dunne?"

Judith's clasped hands tightened in her lap. How do you tell a woman that you believe that her son—her only and frantically adored son—is a psychotic and probably a murderer? She said, "It's about Kyle."

"What about him?" Alarmed belligerence had been growing in the woman's face. For a moment Judith thought that Mrs. Hodge had guessed what she had come here to say. Then she realized it was far more likely that Mrs. Hodge feared to hear something quite different, something like, "Kyle and I are in love," or even, "I am going to have Kyle's baby."

Judith said, "It is very hard to tell you this, but I think your son is ill."

Relief and incredulity mingled in Mrs. Hodge's face. "Ill! Why, except for a cold now and then, Kyle has never been ill."

"I meant—emotional illness."

Something flickered for a moment in Mrs. Hodge's eyes and then was gone. She said coldly, "What on earth do you mean?"

"It's hard to put into words. I really don't know just how to—" Aware that she was floundering, she stopped speaking for a moment and then said with a rush, "How well did Kyle know my cousin Cecily?"

149

Mrs. Hodge flushed. "Mrs. Grenville? Why, he scarcely knew her at all. You'll have to excuse me, Miss Dunne, but your cousin wasn't the sort my son would want anything to do with."

"I realize what you must have felt about her, Mrs. Hodge, and I don't blame you. I'm sure that to you she must have seemed a thoroughly bad lot. But she *was* beautiful. Are you sure that Kyle had nothing at all to do with her last summer?"

Unmistakable anger in the older woman's face now. "What do you mean, to do with her? Why, they had a speaking acquaintance. And I suppose he admired her looks. I suppose any young man would be more or less dazzled by her. But I'm sure he was never in any way—close to her."

Dazzled by her. Kyle had used the same phrase to describe a plowboy's reaction to Anne Boleyn. Best to drop the subject of Cecily for the moment, Judith decided, and turn to something else. She said, "Do you know that your son has a sort of obsession about Mark Smeaton and Anne Boleyn?" As she spoke she recalled that June afternoon weeks before when she and Kyle had encountered each other at Tower Green, that spot where Anne, with Mark Smeaton and her other alleged lovers already dead, had knelt to the swordsman from Calais.

Judith had thought she might have to explain who Mark Smeaton had been. Mrs. Hodge's prompt and vigorous response proved that she already knew. "That's my sister's doing! When he was a child he'd ask her again and again to tell that old story about all of us being descended from that particular Smeaton, and she would always oblige. And the story probably isn't even true. There are quite a few Smeatons scattered around over England, and probably always have been. Our ancestor at that time was probably some other Smeaton entirely.

But that story has influenced Kyle. It's given him a kind of chip on the shoulder, so that he talks about class injustice and a lot of nonsense like that."

Judith said, very carefully, "Wouldn't you say that he identifies with Mark Smeaton? Perhaps enough so that sometimes he actually thinks he is Mark Smeaton, or a kind of reincarnation of him?"

There was no mistaking the fear in Mrs. Hodge's eyes now. She said, "That is the silliest thing I ever heard of."

Judith leaned forward. "Please, Mrs. Hodge! I know how painful this must be for you. No, that's not true. How could I know what this must be like for you, his mother? But if you love him, you've got to help him. We've both got to help him."

The false indignation drained out of Mrs. Hodge's face, leaving only the fear. She said, "Just what made you come here?"

Judith described Kyle's behavior in Bushey Park the afternoon before. "And of course it made me think of the jingle someone had shoved under my door."

"Jingle? What did it say?"

Reluctantly Judith repeated the lines.

Mrs. Hodge was white to the lips now. "And you think my son wrote that?"

"I feel almost certain he did."

"But what do you think it means?"

"I think it means that to—to the person Kyle sometimes becomes, Cecily and Anne Boleyn were the same woman. He might feel that particularly if she had held great physical attraction for him, and yet had—had used him, or humiliated him."

The older woman's words sounded as if she forced them through a constricted throat. "Are you trying to say my son slept with that—that tramp, and then killed her?"

"No! How can I be sure that anything at all actually happened between them? I'm just saying that I think he wrote that jingle. And I think you'll have to agree that whoever did write it is—sick."

Almost as if she hadn't heard Judith's answer, the older woman said, "You are in that jingle too."

Judith swallowed. "I know."

"He likes and respects you." Plainly all her fear that Kyle might fall in love with this American girl had been swallowed up by a greater terror. "Why should he threaten you?"

"Oh, Kyle likes and respects me. But maybe the other one—" She broke off, reliving the moment when someone she had never known before looked out at her from Kyle's eyes. "Maybe the person he sometimes becomes sees only that I look like Cecily, and like some portraits of Anne Boleyn. Or maybe he feels he has something else against me." She thought of him saying beside the lily pond, "It was because of you that the wisteria vine was cut down, wasn't it?"

Mrs. Hodge said, almost in a whisper, "When that stone nearly fell on you night before last, Kyle was on the roof, right above this apartment."

"You're sure of that?"

"Almost sure. I heard something heavy thud on the roof. Workmen sometimes leave wheelbarrows or buckets filled with cement up there. I guess whoever was on the roof blundered into something like that. Anyway, I went to Kyle's room and saw that he must have left the apartment by the service door. Then about ten minutes later I heard that stone strike, and heard the guards calling out and running up to you—" Her voice trailed off.

"When did Kyle return to this apartment?"

"Not for hours and hours. I kept listening for the sound of him coming down the stairs from the roof and

152

then along the hall, but I heard nothing. Finally I went to bed."

"You mean you think he stayed up on the roof for hours?"

"Probably not. In the service area to the north of the palace, there are almost always tall ladders propped against the wall. He could have climbed down one of them. And from there he could have walked to the car park for his car and then driven away. To London, perhaps. Anyway, he was asleep in his room when I woke up the next morning."

She stopped speaking for a moment and then said in a low, painful voice, "I saw him in London one evening last spring. I'd gone there to meet an old friend so that we could see a revival of *The Desert Song*. Afterwards she took the bus to Shepherd's Bush and I started toward another bus stop to wait for the Waterloo Station bus. Then I saw Kyle walking toward me. I was awfully surprised because when I left him he'd said he was going to stay home and watch the football matches on the telly. I said, 'Why, Kyle!' and stopped right in front of him."

She stopped speaking. Judith said, "Do you mean he didn't seem to know you?"

"Oh, yes! He knew who I was, all right. Before he walked on he even smiled at me in a cold sort of way. But I could tell that at that moment I didn't *mean* anything to him."

"Did you ever mention the incident to him afterward?"

"No." All her defenses had crumbled. "I was afraid. I knew that it—it wasn't really Kyle I saw on the street that night. I think I've known for a long time now that there was something wrong with my boy."

She crossed her arms in front of herself, each hand clutching the opposite elbow. "What are you going to do? Go to the police about my son?"

"No!" Judith rose, crossed to the sofa, and sat down beside Kyle's mother. "Whatever he has done, it is because he is sick. Get him into the hands of doctors first. Oh, the police ought to know that we think that he wrote that threatening jingle, and that you think he was on the roof last night, and all the rest of it. But if he is under medical care, if the doctors have prepared him for what is to happen, his arrest won't be the terrible shock it otherwise might be. And although I don't know much about such matters, I think that his being handled as gently as possible now might give him a better chance of getting well eventually."

Mrs. Hodge's voice was dull. "Then you think I should have my son taken to a psychiatric ward?"

"Let his aunt do it. As a nurse in London hospitals, she must have at least some acquaintance among psychiatrists. And Kyle should be at her place by now, shouldn't he?"

"Yes."

"Then talk to her on the phone. Tell her why you think he should be in the hands of doctors. She's close to Kyle. Surely she can persuade him that he should allow himself to be examined.

"It will be painful for your sister," she went on, "because she must be very fond of Kyle. But even so, it won't be as painful as it would be for you."

After a long moment Mrs. Hodge exhaled a shuddering breath. "All right. I'll telephone Sara."

Too upset to even think of trying to work, Judith drove back to her apartment. She sat beside her living room window, sometimes reading a paragraph or two, sometimes looking out at the main house's rear lawn, where four of the younger offspring of the Children of Emmanuel, three girls and a boy, ran on plump, unsteady legs after orange butterflies. But she wasn't really paying attention to either the book or the gleeful toddlers. All her thoughts were centered on that phone on the table beside the sofa.

A little after five it rang. Swiftly Judith lifted the phone from its cradle. "Hello!"

"I talked to my sister," Mrs. Hodge's tired voice said. "I talked to her for almost an hour. Kyle is out at the moment, having tea with one of the dons from his old college. But when he comes in Sara will talk to him, and if she believes there really is something wrong with him—"

Mrs. Hodge stopped speaking. Judith said gently, "She'll persuade him to submit to examination."

"Yes. Sara says she's sure he will agree. I think so too."

"So do I," Judith said.

16

ONE OF the first things Sara Smeaton had done with the money left to her by her Uncle Albert was to buy this mid-nineteenth-century house in Barnbridge Wells. As soon as she'd done so she had converted the ground floor into a separate flat, now rented to a husband and wife, both teachers at the nearby university. The top floor she reserved for herself, with a second bedroom and what she called an attached loo for the frequent visits of her nephew. Because winters in southern England are mild and summers seldom really hot, she had not bothered to have the old house insulated. But on this late Thursday afternoon in July her living room was stiflingly hot. No breath of air stirred the white net curtains at the window. She saw sweat on her nephew's pale face, and felt it on her own forehead and upper lip.

She said, "Oh, Kyle! Maybe this is all nonsense. If it is you'll have to forgive me, luv, and forgive your poor mum, and that little Dunne girl too." But she had slight hope that it was nonsense. As she spoke haltingly of what her sister had told her on the phone, she had seen, not astonishment or indignation in his face, but a growing horror.

He said, "No, I need help." His gaze left his aunt's homely, distressed face and swept around the familiar room. Unlike his mother's overcrowded parlor, it was a pleasant place, with book shelves along one wall, and surprisingly good prints hanging on the other three. His haggard gaze came back to her face. "You see, for almost four years now I've been having blackouts. Sometimes they are very short. I'll just come to with a feeling that five minutes or so have dropped out of my life. Other times I've found myself in a store, or a theater, or on a street, miles from where I last remember being, and with no idea what I've done for the past four or five hours."

"Oh, Kyle!" Sara Smeaton was crying now. Her large nose looked redder than ever. "Why didn't you tell me about it? I can see why you wouldn't have wanted to tell your mum. But you should have told me."

"I suppose I was afraid," he said dully. "And I kept hoping that the blackouts would just—stop."

But if I've done the things it looks as if I've done, he thought, then it really won't matter if they stop the blackouts. It won't matter because it's already too late. He couldn't say that to his Aunt Sara, though, not when she was looking at him with that hopeful pleading in her small gray eyes.

She said, "Will you let me call Dr. Carlin at St. Agnes Hospital in London? He's the best, luv. I could call him right now, and we could take the eleven o'clock train down to London tonight."

"Yes, please call him."

He got up, went down the hall, and entered the room he had occupied for months at a time during his university years, and for briefer periods both before and since. He sat down on the edge of the single bed, took off his loafers, and then stretched out, hands clasped behind his head. The level rays of the sun struck through the open window beside him, bathing the opposite wall in almost blood-colored light. Against the reddened wall the branchlets of a maple tree outside the window cast a motionless black shadow.

Had he actually slipped a threat, in the form of a grotesque jingle, under Judith Dunne's door? Gentle, talented Judith, who listened, actually listened, when a man talked, her clear brown eyes holding a genuine interest. And, far more terrible, had he tried to kill her the night before last? He thought of how he had suddenly found himself leaping backward out of the taxicab's path on that London street, with no idea of why he happened to be at that particular spot, and no memory of how or when he had left his mother's apartment.

And then, a year ago, Cecily Grenville. His aunt had not been able to repeat exactly that rhyme Judith Dunne had found under her door, but even so, he had realized instantly that its most likely interpretation was that the rhymester had killed Cecily.

Trying to ignore the nausea at the pit of his stomach, he forced his mind back to last August, back to an afternoon when he had dropped into the pub across the road from the palace. With a dizzying leap of his pulses he had seen that Cecily Grenville was there, seated alone at a table against the wall opposite the bar. Always before when he had seen her she had been with some man—her husband, or George Sherill, or someone else.

He had smiled at her, hesitated, and then walked over to her table. She had looked up at him, silky lashes half-veiling her dark eyes and a slight smile curving her full mouth. He asked, "Would you mind terribly if I join you?"

She said, "I'd bloody well mind if you didn't."

In a kind of daze, almost oblivious of the arrivals and departures of other patrons, he sat there with her for nearly two hours. Then she glanced at her watch and said, "Must run. Guesties coming to my house tonight. You'd hate them, so I won't ask you to come too."

They both got to their feet. Cecily said, "But my husband is going to some sort of dinner in the city tomorrow night. If you have nothing better to do, come to my house about eight."

Anticipation was like a tight band around his chest. "I'll be there."

All the next day he worried that he might have misunderstood her, that in the evening he would find himself just one of a dozen or more guests. But when he drove through a pouring rain to The Columns that evening, and turned through the open wrought-iron gates, he saw that no other car stood in the drive. And moments later, when she led him into the living room, he saw that it was empty except for themselves. They drank a little sangria, and Kyle as well as Cecily smoked a joint, although he had never cared much for marijuana. And then they had gone upstairs.

In her big corner bedroom she switched on the overhead light. Hunkered down on her heels on the hearth, she had reached up into the fireplace. She laid a brick beside her on the hearth, then another one. Disconcerted, he stood watching her. When she got to her feet and turned to him, smiling, two green-and-white capsules lay on her outstretched palm. "Be my guest, as the Yanks say."

"What are they?"

"Uppers. Speed. Amphetamine, if you want to be formal about it. One for each of us. They'll make it better."

He said, almost roughly, "We won't need stuff like that!" He reached out and switched off the lamp, leaving the room illuminated only by an arc of light from the hall.

After a moment she gave a low, excited laugh. "Maybe

we won't, at that." In the half-light she again crouched on the hearth. He saw her lift the bricks and restore them to some spot in the fireplace's rear wall. Then she stood up and went into his arms.

In both dreams and daydreams he had possessed her so often that the actual possession, there in her big bed, might well have proved to be a disappointment. Instead he felt a sensual intoxication even greater than he had imagined. And when his desire had spent itself he felt none of the momentary sadness and alienation that, some say, always follows passion. Instead he felt an over-whelming tenderness and gratitude. He stroked her dark hair, and kissed the lovely face dimly visible in the light from the hall, and told her that he loved her, would love her until he died, would ask nothing more than just to spend the rest of his life near her.

And then he saw the amused shine of her eyes, and his words stopped.

She giggled. "You look as if you'd just swallowed a glass of water and then realized it was part laundry bleach."

"Cecily!" It had been a cry of sheer pain.

"Oh, come off it. Who do you think we are? Heloise and Abelard? Lancelot and Guinevere? Taylor and Burton? This was a roll in the hay, that's all."

"Cecily! Don't! Don't talk like that!"

"You're okay. You're even a little better than okay. But you're a long way from the best. You know who's the best? Zack Reeve. He's the one who plays lead guitar with The Nightmares. Now there's a stud!"

He thought of Reeve's green-painted face, writhing body, wailing voice underscored by the guitar's heavy beat. He thought of stories he had heard about Reeve and very young girls. "Cecily, you don't know what you're doing to—"

"Oh, stop it!" She no longer sounded amused, just irritated. "My mistake. For a minute there when you said we wouldn't need the speed, I thought you'd turn out to be something special. But I shouldn't have expected a schoolmaster, even a good-looking one, to be anything but a sanctimonious bore." She turned over on her stomach and pillowed her head on her crossed arms. "Will you please go away now? I want to sleep."

She kept her face turned away all the time he was getting dressed. He went downstairs, took his black oil-skin slicker down from where he had hung it in the closet under the stairs, and put it on. When he stepped outside he saw that the rain was still heavy. He drove to a pub—not the one where he had sat with Cecily the day before, but one nearer the railroad station—and began to drink neat brandy. When, through a drunken haze, he heard the barmaid call out, "Time, ladies and gentlemen," he suddenly knew that he couldn't return to his mother's apartment that night, couldn't bear the thought that tomorrow he might see Cecily Grenville in the village or on the palace grounds. He had a key to his aunt's house in Barnbridge Wells and his room was always ready. He would go there for a day or two.

He had left the pub, gotten into his car, and driven to Barnbridge Wells.

Or had he driven straight there?

He could remember leaving the pub and walking through the rain to his car. But after that there was a gap. The next thing he could remember for sure was a highway sign telling him he was a half-mile from the turnoff to Slough. But he had never equated that memory gap with those blackouts of his. No one could recall in detail a night of heavy drinking, and he'd not only had more brandies than he could recollect, but, earlier in the evening, sangria and marijuana.

It wasn't until this terrible moment, when he lay here staring at that wall—its redness faded to a pale yellow now, like that of a huge, washed-out bloodstain—that he began to wonder if he had really driven straight from that pub to Barnbridge Wells. Perhaps instead he had made a hideous detour—

Footsteps along the short hall. Sara Smeaton stood in the doorway. "I talked to Dr. Carlin. He says he will be at the hospital when you check in."

Kyle said tonelessly, "All right."

"We may not get to the hospital until around four in the morning. You see, the eleven o'clock train from here is a local that originates in Edinburgh. It keeps stopping every twenty minutes or so to drop off mail." She paused. "I nursed Dr. Carlin's mother through pneumonia once. I guess that's why he's willing to meet us at that hour. Just the same, I think it's awfully kind of him."

"Yes, very kind."

How tired his aunt looked, and how flushed, as if her blood pressure were soaring. He had an impulse to say, "Wait. We'll go tomorrow, or the next day." But delay would only bring added strain. The best thing he could do now for his mother and his aunt and everyone else was to place himself in the hands of those hospital psychiatrists—and, if he had done what he feared he had, the hands of the police—as soon as possible.

"Your mum won't be at the hospital to meet us. I persuaded her it would be easier on both you and her if she didn't see you until after Dr. Carlin made his first examination, and we have a better idea of—how you are."

Kyle nodded. Just checking into that hospital would be hard enough, without having to bear the sight of his mother's stricken face. "All right. We'll catch the eleven o'clock."

17

THE MAIL-AND-PASSENGER local, made up of some of the oldest cars owned by British Railways, swayed and jolted through the night. In the second-class compartment he sat with his head back against the seat's worn brown plush and watched Sara Smeaton from narrow eyes. She stared out of the window, her homely, worried face reflected dimly in the glass.

Always after he found himself in control he felt at least a momentary confusion about just where he was. But it was all straight in his head now. He remembered how that poor sod Kyle had entered this empty compartment with Sara Smeaton about an hour ago. He remembered how Kyle, before that, had been on the bed in old lady Smeaton's flat, agonizing over what he might have done to that Grenville bitch. He remembered that still earlier Kyle had sat in his aunt's living room, sweating from every pore as she told him about her conversation with his mother.

Yes, he had it all straight now. True, there was always that basic confusion in his mind, the one concerning just who he was. Sometimes it seemed to him that he was reliving bits of the life of Mark Smeaton, that ancestor that everyone had done the dirty on. But often he knew exactly where he was in both time and space. He glanced at the watch strapped to his wrist. Right now, for in-

stance, he knew that it was twelve-thirty Thursday night
—or rather, Friday morning—and that in a few moments the train would come to a jerky halt at a village called Lower Tutnam.

And anyway, if sometimes he felt a slight confusion about who he was, he at all times knew who he was *not*. He was not Kyle Hodge, that poor twerp who was too stupid even to know that he shared a body with someone twice as bright and strong and ruthless as himself.

Oh, not that poor old Kyle couldn't lose his temper, and even hit out, but only on behalf of someone else. Because of that sniveling cockney brat, for instance, he'd split the Latin master's lip and gotten himself sacked. But he had been ready to take the sneering things Cecily Grenville said, just take them and slink away.

Fortunately he himself had been able to seize control almost as soon as Kyle left the pub that rainy night last August. He did not feel the drunkenness that Kyle had been experiencing only seconds before. Perhaps it was the guilt the poor goody-goody felt over anything stronger than ale that gave him such a poor head for liquor. Anyway, he himself felt just high enough to make the thought of what he was going to do doubly enjoyable. He remembered stopping the car to take driving gloves from the compartment in the dash and put them on. Then he drove through the heavy rain to The Columns.

He found the gates still open, the front door unlocked, and a lamp on in the living room. Its light shone down on almost empty glasses of sangria and on crumpled brown stubs in an ashtray. The air was still faintly redolent of pot. He returned to the center hall and walked down it until he came to the partially open door of the kitchen. He touched a switch. Light gleamed on tile and porcelain and stainless steel. In the third of the counter drawers he opened he found what he was looking for.

Cleaver in hand, he mounted the stairs to the lighted upper hall. When he slipped quietly into the corner room through the half-open door he saw that the sleeping girl had moved very little since Kyle had left her. She still lay on her stomach, left arm crooked between her cheek and the pillow, right arm extended straight out from the shoulder over the light yellow blanket.

He set to work swiftly and savagely. Evidently the first blow killed her because the only sound she made was a kind of explosive sigh, as if the shock of that first blow had expelled all the air from her lungs.

Finally he stepped back from the bed. Even with his back to the light from the hall he could see that there was blood on his slicker. But no matter. Rain would wash the blood away, and the slicker must have protected the rest of his clothing. As for the cleaver, he could throw it in the river.

Suddenly he realized he didn't want to throw it away. Nor did he have to. He could leave it here. It wouldn't matter if it was found. There were no fingerprints on it. And if it weren't found, later on he could come back here and take it from its hiding place—

Still wearing his gloves, he went into the adjoining bathroom, switched on the light, and washed the cleaver blade and handle. He came back into the bedroom and crouched before the fireplace. Seconds later a plastic bottle of amphetamine capsules was in his pocket, and the cleaver was hidden behind the bricks.

He went rapidly down the stairs, out onto the front lawn, and stood there for several minutes under the torrent of rain. Then he got into the car, drove back to the sleeping village, and out onto the bridge. Halfway over he stopped, walked to the balustrade, and threw both the bloodstained driving gloves into the Thames. Then he continued driving north.

Near Slough he felt Kyle trying to take over. He did not mind. He himself was tired by then. He moved into his own small corner of consciousness, that corner that Kyle, the poor fool, did not even know existed. As always at such moments he noted with amusement how confused and anxious Kyle felt, how puzzled at finding himself miles from where he last remembered being. Tonight, though, the poor slob was able to tell himself that his trouble was nothing but a lot of brandy taken on top of sangria and pot.

He did not attempt to wrest control from Kyle all during the weeks the police were actively investigating Cecily's murder. By October, though, the police had all but given up. True, they had found scores of fingerprints all over the house, including that corner room. But many of them were too smudged to be of any use, others did not correspond with those of Cecily's known associates or with any prints in the police files, and those which were both unsmudged and traceable belonged to persons who could account for all their movements the night of the crime.

In early November he paid the first of his several visits to that now-uninhabited house. After driving his car off the road into the shelter of a clump of trees, he walked half a mile to The Columns. The gates were locked. Leaping high, he grasped the coping at the top of the brick wall, drew himself up, and dropped into the long grass on the other side. He stopped for a few moments to draw on the thin rubber gloves he had taken from a drawer in Millie Hodge's kitchen. Then he moved toward the house.

As he had expected to, he found all the doors locked. Nor could he hope to get past the protective grilles at the long windows. But in circling the house he had noticed the ancient wisteria vine espalliered against the north wall. He climbed it. As he had hoped, that upstairs window was unlocked. Inside the room he played the beam of a pocket torch over the now-empty corner where the big bed had stood, over the white scatter rugs which, he was sure, covered lingering traces of bloodstains, over the fireplace's white brick face.

He laid the torch, still lighted, on top of the chest of drawers. From a jacket pocket he took a stubby candle and the metal lid of a jar which once had held pickles. These two items also had come from the kitchen of that grace-and-favor apartment. He lighted the wick and let enough wax drip on the metal cap to hold the candle upright. He placed the lighted candle on the chest of drawers, switched off the torch, and crossed the room to crouch down on the hearth. Yes, the cleaver was still in its hiding place. He had thought that was the case, because there had been no word of the weapon's discovery in the newspapers. Still, knowing for sure that the police had not found it sent a marvelous sense of omnipotence surging through him.

Cleaver in hand, he walked over to where the bed had once stood. He had hoped that by coming here he could relive his vengeance upon Cecily, almost as vividly as he had experienced it that night last August. But for some reason, perhaps the absence of the bed, he could not conjure up the image of her lying on it. Well, no matter. It had happened *once*. He went over to the chaise longue and sat down. Through candlelight that sometimes flickered in draughts moving up the stairwell and along the hallway, he looked around the room and thought of how Kyle, if he knew, ought to be grateful to him for avenging the Grenville woman's insults. Not that he would be, of course. He grinned at the thought of what that poor, windmill-tilting fool would feel if he learned that his own hands had wielded that cleaver.

After awhile he blew out the candle and dropped both it and the metal jar cap into his pocket. By the light of his pocket torch he restored the cleaver to its place. Then he descended the wisteria vine to the ground and went back to his car.

Twice more during the winter he had visited the corner room. Then, last June, that nosy American bitch had somehow guessed that someone had been in the house, and told Grenville about it. He was sure that was what had happened, because it was right after Judith Dunne had come back to stay in that apartment that Grenville had taken the vine down. Well, he'd gotten even with her for that. How that jingle must have made her hair stand up!

He had thought of signing his composition "M." That was how he thought of himself. Just M. It stood for Mack the Knife of *The Threepenny Opera*. It also stood for the title of a famous German film about a murderer, a picture he hoped to see someday. And it stood for Mark. Oh, not that he was anything like the stupid patsy that Mark Smeaton had been, first for the woman and then for the man who had wanted to get rid of her. Nevertheless, he felt that part of him *was* Mark Smeaton, a Smeaton as tough and vengeful as he had once been soft-headed and soft-hearted.

Finally, though, he had left the jingle unsigned. That way, he felt, there would be a better chance that she would think Grenville or someone else had written it.

That business with the capstone had been almost a spur-of-the-moment idea. While sun-bathing up on the palace roof the previous afternoon he—or rather, both he and Kyle, for Kyle was in control then—had noticed that the capstone looked loose. Kyle, of course, had made a mental note to report the matter to Steven Grenville or the foreman of the palace masons, whichever one he encountered first. He himself had been reminded of the loose bricks in the fireplace of that room, and of the girl who had put a stop to his visiting that house.

Past nine the next evening, moving along a path that led up from the Thames, Kyle had seen Judith sitting on a bench outside the palace's east front. The poor dope had started toward her eagerly. Although she wasn't the obsession with him that her cousin had been, Kyle was more than a little in love with the American girl. But before Kyle could reach her, he himself had been able to take over. Changing course, he had gone back through the palace's Fountain Court and Clock Court to Base Court, and from there up three flights of stairs to the roof. Judith, surely, would be coming through Base Court soon on her way to the car park. And in the growing darkness she would keep to the surer footing of the walk that ran close to the palace wall. With both hands he rocked the loose capstone back and forth and then just stood with legs braced, waiting.

He had not tried particularly to hit her. Oh, he would not have minded if he had. But he had been content just to give her another good scare.

Now, though, he thought grimly, everything was different. Now he owed her all he had owed Cecily Grenville, and more besides. Because Judith Dunne was trying to see to it that he was locked up, either in a prison or a psycho ward.

The train slowed for the Lower Tutnam station and then came to a jerky stop. He waited, listening to the thud of mail bags on the station platform, and willing that no new passenger would open the compartment door. His luck held. As the train pulled away from the station, he and Sara Smeaton were still the compartment's only occupants. She turned and give him a tired smile. He returned the smile. Then she leaned her graying head against the back rest. After a few moments her jaw dropped and she began to snore the loud snores of almost total exhaustion.

Best not to wait any longer. The next station served a much larger town, and there was a chance that even at this hour a number of people, at least one of whom might enter this compartment, would be waiting on the platform. Besides, if he remembered this area correctly, this would be a good place to leave the train.

He took the ticket stub the conductor had slipped under the metal holder affixed to the back of the seat and placed it in his pocket. Then he went out into the empty, murkily lit corridor and pulled the emergency cord.

The train came to a screeching halt. He went back into the compartment and opened its outer door. He could see the graveled roadbed about three feet below, sloping toward a weed-choked ditch.

"Kyle!" Sara Smeaton had reached up to clutch his arm. "What are you doing?" Terror in her face, she stood up.

With a backward sweep of his arm he brought the edge of his hand against her throat. She fell full length on the compartment floor. Without looking back at her he jumped down to the gravel and then, reaching up, closed the compartment door.

Aware of the roaring in her head, Sara Smeaton knew what was happening to her. But no matter. The important thing was that somebody stop Kyle. No, not Kyle. It was not Kyle who had given her a fleeting look and then knocked her to the floor.

She managed to roll over to her hands and knees. Reaching up, she grasped the handle of the half-open door to the corridor and pulled herself partway erect. The door slid further in its grooves, and, with the handle slipping out of her grasp, she fell half-in, half-out of the compartment. By then footsteps were ringing across the car's steel vestibule but she did not know it. All sound was blotted out by the roaring in her head.

The two uniformed trainmen stopped at sight of her. Then the elder of them knelt beside her on the corridor floor. He looked at the fixed stare in the little gray eyes, the twisted face. "Stroke," he said.

"You're sure?"

"Ought to be. I've seen three strokes in my own family." He turned his head and looked into the compartment. "She felt it coming on, see, so she came out here and pulled the emergency cord. Then the stroke hit her." He paused. "You worked this car. Did she have anyone with her?"

The younger man frowned. "Seems to me she got on at Barnbridge Wells and that there was a young chap with her." He sidled past his colleague and the stricken woman into the compartment. "Yes, here's her stub in the holder. Barnbridge Wells to London. But I don't see a stub for him. Guess he got off back there at Lower Tutnam."

"Well, one thing's certain. This poor woman won't be able to tell us, at least not for some time. Thank God our next stop is Gorman. They've got a hospital there. Now the engine driver must have sent someone back to find out what's wrong. Why don't you walk through the cars and meet him?"

Before he stopped to get his bearings, he had put several hundred feet between himself and the halted train, first rolling under the lowest strand of a wire fence beyond the ditch, and then moving as rapidly as possible across a meadow of knee-high grass. Finally he circled a spinney of broad-leafed trees and then stopped to catch his breath. In the distance he heard the train start up.

Soon the throb of its engine and the clatter of its cars dwindled to silence.

The only illumination was starlight. But then, he had good night vision. Fairly confident that he would not blunder into a ditch or a wooden cattle trough, he headed in what he judged to be the direction of the nearest highway.

About twenty minutes later he reached it. At this hour only a few cars moved along it. He waited until there were no cars in sight and then crossed to more open fields. Ahead a line of trees marked a country road. If he remembered correctly from the two times that he—or rather, Kyle—had driven along that road, it led to an area of big, widely spaced houses, many extremely modern in design, and occupied by the talented and successful— aerospace engineers from a government-owned plant twenty miles away, and actors and writers and directors employed by England's second-largest film studio, only fifteen miles away.

He reached the road. Keeping at its edge and stopping in the shadow of trees whenever he heard a car approaching from either direction, he soon came to the first of the big houses, a fake Tudor set back behind an iron picket fence. The house was completely dark. The next two houses had a few lights showing, but it wasn't until he reach the fourth that he found what he wanted, a party still in full swing. Light and music poured from the big white cement house with its central tower flanked by ells with sharply angled roofs. Cars filled the circular drive. More cars, probably those of late arrivals, lined the road.

Perhaps some of those late arrivers were extremely careless or, if they had first attended another party, extremely high. Whatever the reason, he found the key in the ignition of the first car he inspected, a black Jaguar two-seater. He got in, started the engine, and drove off in the direction the Jaguar had been pointed, south.

Behind an open window in the main house a baby began to cry. The sound, plus the sudden glare of a ceiling light over there, so strong that it shone into her own window, brought Judith awake. Even after the crying stopped and the light went out, she remained awake and strangely ill at ease. She wondered why. What was frightening about a baby awakened by a tummy ache or a bad dream? Why should she be afraid of anything with all those Children of Emmanuel only a few yards away? And yet she had a sense of some onrushing disaster.

The last time she looked at the luminous dial of her bedside clock its hands pointed to three. She went back to sleep soon after that.

18

HE WAS still about five miles from Hampton Court when he became aware that, even though a few stars still shone in the sky's zenith, the eastern horizon had grayed with dawn. Miss Judith Dunne would just have to wait for what was coming to her. It would be light soon, and his chance of slipping past that houseful of religious nuts—most of them early risers, probably—would be poor. Better to hole up for a few hours in that spot he'd thought of soon after he stole the Jaguar.

A few minutes later he could make out Bushey Park's brick wall beyond oaks and lindens at the road's left-hand side. Then the headlights' refracted glow showed him a group of English willows. Good. Parked in among those thick trailing branches, the Jaguar might go unnoticed indefinitely. And even if a police patrol along this road did see it, they would not bother to investigate the car until it had stood there for twenty-four hours or so longer.

He ran the Jaguar in among the willows and then sat there for a moment, thinking. The park wall was higher than that surrounding the Grenville house, perhaps too high for him to scale it if he started from the ground. After a moment he restarted the car, backed up, and then drove forward, pulling in as close as possible to the wall. After pocketing the ignition key he climbed onto the car's hood. From there he found it easy to pull himself up onto the wall and then drop into the long, dew-wet grass on the other side. He moved across the park toward the palace.

He had just passed the Diana Fountain when he saw a guard, a member of Hampton Court's night patrol, moving toward him. "Good morning, Mr. Hodge. Up early, I see."

The guard was looking at his shoes. He too looked down, and saw that they were heavily caked with mud. Also there was a rip in his right trouser leg, just above the cuff. The mud must have come from those meadows he crossed after he left the train. As for the tear, perhaps that had happened as he went over the Bushey Park wall. He said, "At the first party I was at tonight—I mean last night—there was this New Orleans jazz combo and somebody got the idea they should lead us in a march across the fields. Or was that the second party?"

The guard laughed and started to move away. "Just as long as you're home in one piece. That's what I used to say when I was your age."

He looked after the guard for a moment. Then, careful not to hurry his steps, he went on several hundred yards beside a high yew hedge and then turned through an archway, cut out of the shrubbery, into the service area along the palace's north wall. As usual, workmen had left aluminum ladders, extended to various lengths, propped against the wall. He chose one of them and moved it a couple of feet so that it would give him easy access to one of the casement windows. Beyond that window was an apartment which had remained empty ever since the death of its last tenant, Lady Strickland, more than a month earlier.

He bent, picked up a jagged piece of brick, and put it in his jacket pocket. For a second or two he looked carefully in both directions. Then, hurrying now, he climbed the ladder. When he reached the window with its many small leaded panes he used the brick to break a pane beside the window's fastening. The glass broke cleanly, leaving only one small shard portruding from the frame. To him the noise seemed loud in the silence, but he knew than in reality it was less loud than the dawn chorus of starlings, robins, and other birds sounding from everywhere on the palace grounds. He reached in through the space where the pane had been, depressed a handle, and swung the window back.

Once inside the room he turned, leaned out, and shifted the light ladder so that it no longer rose directly to where he stood. Then, swiftly and quietly, he closed the window. Days might pass before anyone noticed that, out of the thousand of palace windows, this one had a pane missing, and even more days might pass before the damage was repaired.

He looked around him through the dim light. No furniture in this room nor, as far as he could see through an open doorway, any in the next room, either. But no matter. In one corner was a stack of what looked like folded draperies, long ones of deep brown velvet. He rearranged them so that they formed a mat sufficiently wide and several inches thick. Then he lay down and almost immediately fell asleep.

Dr. Charles Islan, tall and red-haired and two days short of his thirtieth birthday, unhooked the chart from the foot of the woman's hospital bed and looked at it. "Smeaton, Sara. So that's her name." When she had been brought into the Gorman hospital four hours earlier, he had set to work immediately—giving an injection to bring down her blood pressure, testing to make sure which hemisphere of her brain had been damaged—

without knowing anything about her except that she had been stricken aboard a train. "Have her relatives been notified?"

The nurse straightened the fold of sheet and blanket across the patient's chest. "As far as I know, sir, they haven't yet learned who her relatives are. All the identification in her purse gave was her name, and some address and telephone number in Barnbridge Wells. Nobody answered the phone at that number."

"Well, sooner or later we'll find her family, if she has one."

He looked at the patient. The small gray eyes in the paralysis-distorted face no longer stared emptily. Instead he had a sense that an imprisoned Sara Smeaton was trying desperately to communicate with him. Communicate what? The fear that any such patient must feel? No, it was not just that. She was trying to tell him something, warn him about something. Well, the poor woman would not be able to do so, not until, or if, the damaged speech center in the left half of her brain recovered sufficiently to allow her to form words, either vocally or in writing. He placed the chart on its hook and turned away.

When she awoke, Judith saw by the clock beside her bed that it was almost eleven. She lay back and stared dully at the ceiling. Perhaps because of that wakeful period in the early morning hours, or of the troubled dreams—dreams she could not remember—which had preceded and followed it, she felt even more tired than she had before she went to sleep.

She thought of Kyle, and of his poor mother, and of that nice, homely aunt of his. She thought of Steven Grenville. And she wished fervently that she had not come back to England this summer.

Because she was humanly selfish, it was the thought of Steven which oppressed her most—or rather, the thought of what Steven must think of her. And it all might have been so different. He was attracted to her—perhaps had been from their first meeting more than a year ago—just as she had been attracted to him. But she had suspected him of contriving his own wife's murder. She had suspected him of sending that section of Portland stone off the roof to smash in Base Court. And she had let him see what she suspected. No wonder his voice had sounded cold and hard, even scornful, the last time they had talked on the phone.

Suddenly she knew what she should do. Go back to New York right away. Tomorrow, if she could get a plane seat. After all, she had only one more drawing to do, one of obese and gouty Queen Anne, the last of the Stuart monarchs.

Once back in New York with Barney, she gradually would forget how stupidly she had behaved this summer. With Barney, after awhile she would stop wondering what her life might have been like with that tall man with the gray eyes and strong-planed face.

The phone rang. Not bothering to put on a robe, she went into the living room in her nightgown and lifted the phone from its cradle.

It was Mrs. Hodge, her voice hoarse with fatigue and strain. "Judith?" Sometime during their conversation of the afternoon before she had stopped calling Judith Miss Dunne. "I've been watching from my window, but I didn't see you. Aren't you coming to the palace today?"

"Yes, this afternoon." She paused. "Have you had any word of Kyle?"

"No. But Sara said it might be a good many hours before she had—anything definite to tell me. Judith, could you stop by and see me before you start work on your drawing? It's nothing special. I just thought we might talk."

Judith understood. Frightened and grieving, Kyle's mother needed company. "All right. I should be there around two o'clock."

When she had hung up she sat there with her hand on the phone. Would Steven be in his office now? Perhaps. He had said that he was returning on Friday. And if she intended to leave the next day, she should tell him so. In a sense, he was her landlord. She looked up his office number and dialed.

Miss Claverly answered. A moment later Judith was speaking to Steven. "I wanted to tell you that I'm going back to New York. Tomorrow, if I can manage it."

After a moment he said, in a completely neutral tone, "Oh?"

"Yes. I'll have finished my work here by late this afternoon, so there seems to be no point in staying. If Miss Claverly will order the utilities turned off and then mail me the bills, I'll send a check." She knew she was chattering but she didn't know how to stop. "I'm sorry to give you such short notice, but then it isn't as if I were your tenant in the usual sense, is it?"

He said, in that same level voice, "You're not my tenant in any sense. You've been staying there under the terms of my wife's will."

"About Cecily," Judith said, and then stopped.

"Yes?"

"Forgive me for ever having thought that—that you had anything to do with what happened to her."

After a moment he asked, "You're sure now that I did not?"

"Yes."

"Why are you sure?"

"Because—" She broke off. She liked Kyle. Besides,

she could not know exactly what he had done, or rather, what that other person she had glimpsed looking out of his eyes had done. That was for the psychiatrists to determine, and the police.

She said, "I'm sure, that's all."

"I see." If his tone had become warmer, she could not perceive it.

Silence. Obviously he was waiting for her to hang up. "Goodbye," she said. She replaced the phone and then just sat there for several moments. Finally she dressed and went into the kitchen to make her belated breakfast.

It was a little past two when she turned into the main gate to the palace grounds and drove past the grandstand. It was ready for tonight's sound and light show now, with a ticket booth set up inside a fence of steel mesh. She left the Volvo in the car park, crossed the moat bridge to Base Court, and climbed to the Hodge apartment.

For over an hour she sat in that fussy parlor, looking at album snapshots of Kyle from the age of a few months on, and listening to his mother's stories of how handsome he had always been, and how intelligent and loving. "And yet it's as I told you, Judith. For several years I've felt from time to time that Kyle just—went away. I would be right in the same room with him, and everything would be as always, and then suddenly, perhaps for only a few minutes, it would be as if someone else was sitting there in his chair."

As she spoke, Mrs. Hodge's eyes kept going to the phone. Once it rang, and she lifted it with a hand that trembled visibly. But the call was a wrong number.

Judith felt a growing sadness. Sadness for Kyle, and the two aging women who loved him. Sadness for herself, because she would be going back to New York tomorrow and back to Barney who—she faced it now—

never had attracted her as much as stiff-necked, bluntly honest Steven Grenville did.

At last she said, "I really must go, Mrs. Hodge. As it is, I may have to finish my drawing by artificial light."

"Will you come back here for a bite to eat when you've finished?"

"That may not be until nine o'clock, or even later."

"That will be all right. Perhaps I'll have had some word from my sister by then."

"Very well," Judith said, trying to hide her reluctance. "I'll be here." She left the apartment and descended the worn stairs.

When she emerged into Base Court she saw George Sherill moving toward her across the brick pavement. She said, "Are you all set for the sound and light show?"

"Yes, thank God. Do you plan to see it?"

"No. I intend to work as late as possible in the State Apartments."

"Well, the thing is going to run for ten nights, heaven help us all, so you'll have plenty of chances to see it."

In no mood to prolong the conversation, she did not tell him that by tomorrow night she would be in New York. "Well, goodbye," she said, and moved on across the courtyard.

Dr. Gilbert Carlin, assistant chief of psychiatry at London's St. Agnes Hospital, drove down Sloane Street through the mid-afternoon sunlight toward his flat in Belgravia. Fatigue far greater than he usually felt at the end of his day's stint at St. Agnes had deepened lines in his face, so that he looked older than his forty-seven years. His tiredness, he knew, was due to the fact that he had risen before dawn in order to be at the hospital when Sara Smeaton and her nephew arrived. To his puzzled chagrin, they had never turned up.

He had intended to call Sara Smeaton's flat in Barn-bridge Wells as soon as he finished his breakfast in the hospital's staff dining room, but a crisis on Ward D had interfered. One of the patients had managed to kindle a fire in a wastebasket, thereby upsetting several other patients. More than three hours had passed before the ward was reasonably quiet again. Thus it was almost noon before he had been able to call Sara Smeaton's number.

There had been no answer. Frowning, he had hung up. It was not like the woman he remembered to alter her plans capriciously, especially when others would be inconvenienced by the unannounced change. Further-more, she had sounded distressed indeed when she had talked to him over the phone the evening before. She had reason to think, she said, that her nephew was not only mentally ill, but dangerously so.

He did not know the nephew's name. Presumably it was not Smeaton, since she had referred to him as "my sister's son." And all he had gathered about the sister was that she lived somewhere in the London area.

Well, perhaps Nurse Smeaton and her nephew had been unable to catch last night's train, although why she had not called his flat to tell him so he could not imagine. But anyway, perhaps they were on their way to the hospital now. As soon as he'd had a nap, he would phone the hospital. If they still had not arrived, he would again phone the Smeaton flat in Barnbridge Wells. And if by early evening he had not made contact with Sara Smea-ton, he would ask for police assistance in finding her and her nephew.

He turned off onto a quiet, tree-shadowed street and stopped his car at the foot of stone steps leading up to one of a row of handsome Georgian houses, long since con-verted into flats.

19

WITH A START, Kyle awoke and sat bolt upright in the dimming light. Where was he? Why had been lying asleep on—Yes, it was a pile of outspread window draperies.

Enough daylight remained so that, after a moment, he could make out the medallion pattern of the green-and-gold flecked wallpaper. He knew then that he was in the dining room of what had been Lady Strickland's apartment. He had seen that wallpaper one day last summer when, emerging from his mother's apartment, he had observed an overaged delivery man trying to maneuver a liquor cabinet through Lady Strickland's doorway. He had helped the man carry the cabinet into the flat and set it down in this room.

Caked mud on his shoes. A tear in his right trouser leg. How had that happened?

Trying to stave off panic, he looked at his watch. Eight-forty. A.M. or P.M.? He turned his head and looked at the light coming through the casement window. Evening light, surely.

A broken pane, there near the handle of the window fastening. So that was how he had gotten in.

Panic overwhelmed him then. He remembered lying on that familiar bed in his aunt's house, staring at a sunset-reddened wall. He remembered boarding the train with his aunt, and sitting with her in a second-class compartment for—how long? Twenty minutes? Half an hour? All he knew for sure was that the memory of that train ride abruptly gave way to blankness, like a movie screen when the film has broken. The only difference was that the blankness did not resemble the glaring white of a movie screen. Instead it was a sudden darkness in his mind.

What had happened during that dark interval? Where had he gone? What had he done? And his aunt. Where was she? In his last memory of her she had been seated opposite him in the shabby compartment, smiling at him now and then, but most of the time staring out the window into the darkness. Oh, God! Had he left the train soon after that? And had he done something to her before he left, something to keep her from having him followed?

Nausea in the pit of his stomach now, and in his ears a swift pounding that, after a moment, he recognized as the surge of his heartbeats. He knew that he must give himself up, and not just to some hospital psychiatrist. He must walk out of the palace and across the bridge over the Thames and into the police station, and ask them to lock him up.

But he could not, just yet. He could not even get to his feet. His whole body felt sore and sensitive, as if his nerve ends were protected now by only the thinnest layer of skin.

In the salon bar of a pub near his flat Steven Grenville placed his knife and fork at the outer edge of his plate and then frowned down at his half-finished steak-and-kidney pie. There was nothing wrong with the pie. It was just that the memory of his last phone conversation with Judith had taken away his appetite.

He ought to be glad she was returning to New York. Her presence this summer had caused him considerable turmoil. Because she was his dead wife's cousin, she had brought him constant reminder of Cecily. Because he was attracted to her, her obvious suspicion of him had been galling indeed. Nevertheless, he had succumbed to his need to be with her and had taken her out several times. Then, just when he had begun to think they might have a future together, he and this girl who looked so much like Cecily and in reality was so very different from her, he found that her distrust of him had decreased not one whit.

Until now.

Again he went over that last conversation with her. She was now "sure," she had said, that he'd had no part in Cecily's death. When he had asked her, coldly, why she was sure, she had hesitated for a moment and then said something like, "I'm just sure, that's all."

At the time he had thought that Judith, womanlike, was asserting her belief in her intuition—an intuition that, likely as not, might tell her in a few days or weeks that he was guilty as sin. But now a new thought struck him. What if she had run across some sort of evidence that had convinced her beyond doubt of his innocence? About the only form that evidence could take would be proof that it was someone else who had invaded Cecily's room that night and killed her with a kitchen cleaver.

Coldness rippled down his spine. Judith was so ingenuous, so incapable of hiding what she thought or felt. If she knew the identity of the wielder of that kitchen cleaver, had she allowed him to guess what she had learned? If so, she might at this moment be in danger.

He pushed back his chair, crossed the cosy room with

its half-dozen diners in high-backed booths, and, at the pay phone in one corner, dialed Judith's number. No answer.

He hung up. Had she said she was going to the palace today? If so, she might still be there. He could not remember exactly what she had said, but it seemed to him that she had implied she had some drawing to complete before she returned to New York.

He stood there in an agony of indecision. If she were still at the palace, then going to her apartment would be a waste of perhaps precious time. On the other hand, if she were lying in one of those rooms above the carriage house, badly injured or perhaps even dying—

Coming to a sudden decision, he turned away from the phone. He left a pound note and some coins beside the remains of his steak-and-kidney pie and hurried out to his car.

In the Queen's Drawing Room on the eastern side of the palace Judith laid down her charcoal pencil and then stepped back from the easel. In the sketch Queen Anne sat in a high-backed chair, her stubborn gaze fixed on the man who stood before her, one hand held out in a pleading gesture.

The man was Antonio Verrio, an eighteenth-century painter whom many people, including Judith, considered to have been not very good. Nevertheless, he deserved to be treated far better than he had been. He had painted many walls and ceilings in the State Apartments, including the ceiling of this splendid room. Always he'd had to plead for money from his royal clients, and nearly always he'd had to settle for less than he was owed. In the sketch on the easel he pleaded for enough money to buy the paints necessary to finish his work in this very room.

In Judith's depressed state she felt it only fitting that her last drawing at Hampton Court should depict one of the palace's least attractive tenants. Poor Queen Anne—fat, gluttonous, and afflicted not only by gout and miscarriages but a chronically tight fist.

An hour ago, as the light began to fade, Judith had moved aside a small ornamental plaque one of the guards had pointed out to her, touched the switch the plaque covered, and thus turned on the large electric floodlight concealed by the eighteenth-century crystal chandelier. She knew that outside it must be dark now, or nearly so. Several hundred yards away, on the lawn facing the palace's western front, the audience would be filing into the grandstand for the sound and light show. Perhaps the performance had already begun. When she first heard about the coming spectacle, Judith had been eager to attend. Now she felt too depressed to want to do anything except place her drawing in her case, turn out the light, and go home to pack for the next day's flight to New York.

Then she remembered that she had promised Mrs. Hodge to stop by for "a bite to eat." That meant that she could not simply walk out the palace's eastern exit, circle around to the administrative car park, and then drive to The Columns. Instead she would have to walk back through the palace to Base Court and climb to Mrs. Hodge's apartment. Well, so be it. Dispirited as she herself felt, she could not break her promise to that poor woman.

20

THE DINING ROOM of the empty apartment was almost completely dark now. Slowly Kyle Hodge got to his feet. He would go down to the river, he had decided, before he went to the police station. He'd always loved a particular spot on the river bank, just east of the Banqueting House, where weeping willows trailed their branches in the silently flowing water. After an interval there, perhaps, he would feel strong enough to walk into the station calmly and even with a measure of dignity.

Just as in his mother's apartment, there was an automatic lock on the front door. He turned the latch, stepped out in the lighted corridor, and then closed the door behind him. For a moment he looked longingly down the hall to his mother's door. But no. Seeing her now would unnerve him completely.

He went down the stairs to Base Court and then halted in bewilderment. Somewhere a man was singing to the accompaniment of a lute. He recognized the archaically worded verses. They were some that Henry the Eighth had written. Of course! This must be Friday night and—

He was unable to finish the thought. He felt vertigo, and then a sense of spiraling down and down into blackness.

*   *   *

That other one stood motionless, feeling more than the usual confusion that beset him whenever he first came into control. The sound of a lute and a man's voice singing seemed to come from all over.

The singing stopped. The last note of the lute hung vibrating in the air for a moment and then died. That masculine voice that seemed to come from all over said fervently, "And by the rood, as my name is Harry Tudor, I meant every word of it."

A young woman's musical laughter rang out. "By the rood, as my name is Nan Bullen, I do not believe a word of it."

Standing there in Base Court he felt a heady surge of triumph. Nan Bullen, the name Anne Boleyn was known by to many. So she was still alive, and fat Henry was courting her, and it all still lay in the future—their marriage, and Henry's disenchantment with her, and her cold-blooded scheme to get herself pregnant, no matter what risks to the man involved. But this time, he resolved fiercely, everything would be different. This time she would not find she was dealing with a helpless, moonstruck fool—

Someone was moving toward him through the deepening dark. A woman, walking swiftly and lightly. Anne?

Then, as she drew closer, time straightened itself out. This was the late twentieth century, not the early sixteenth. That music—because the actor was singing again—was pouring out of concealed loudspeakers as part of a tourist attraction called a sound and light show. And the girl moving toward him, although almost as dangerous to him as Anne had been to Mark, was someone quite different, a sly, nosy little American.

The girl had seen him now. She halted. As an animal might have, he could almost smell her surprise and fear.

Heart swelling with exultance, he moved casually toward her. Careful, he warned himself. Don't do anything to make her scream, or move in the wrong direction. He stopped and stood still.

She said uncertainly, "Kyle?"

"Hello, Judith. Is something wrong?"

"It's just that I'm surprised to see you here. I thought you'd gone to visit your aunt."

Filthy, lying little bitch. As if she didn't know anything about the plot against him, when it was she who had talked his mother, and indirectly his aunt, into trying to have him locked up. He said, "I did go up to Barnbridge Wells, but I've been feeling rather strange lately, so my aunt suggested we go to see a doctor she knows at this hospital in London. He wants me to come back tomorrow, so he can complete his examination."

She looked at him uncertainly. Was it really with the knowledge and consent of a psychiatrist, not to mention his mother and aunt, that he stood here free and unattended? It must be. And yet—

If only it were light enough for her to see his face clearly. Then she might be sure whether or not it was Kyle who stood there.

Get out of here, a voice inside her said. Get out, and go home, and lock and bolt the door, and then call someone—Steven, or the police, or both. Better yet, drive straight to the police station.

"Well, goodnight, Kyle." She started past him.

"Not that way." He stopped himself, just in time, from reaching out and seizing her arm. "You can't get out over Moat Bridge because they put up a steel folding gate across the west entrance just before the sound and light show started." Not true, probably. Probably there were only the usual nighttime guards at the palace entrance.

But the chances were overwhelming that she wouldn't know that.

She had halted. He said, with a chuckle, "And even if you did get out that way, you'd find yourself facing all those people in the grandstand. You'd spoil the illusion for them. Best to walk back to the East Front and leave the palace that way."

The voice of the actor who played Henry the Eighth was pouring out of the loudspeakers again, angry now, demanding a divorce. He was answered by the dignified, quietly defiant voice of the actress playing his first wife, Catherine of Aragon. Through the sounds of their quarrel Judith spoke, her own voice swift and breathy with fear. "All right. I'll go out that way. Goodnight, Kyle."

She turned and moved rapidly across the paving and through the arch into the next courtyard. He made no move to follow. He knew which way she would turn once she was onto the palace grounds—left, and then left again, toward the car park. Nor did he have to worry about her getting too far ahead of him. Once he was out in the darkness he would have no trouble catching up with her.

She ought to be nearing the exit in the palace's East Front by now. Swiftly and noiselessly he moved after her.

21

THE GUARD at the palace's eastern exit said, "Good evening, Mr. Hodge."

"Good evening. I thought I'd take a stroll."

The guard chuckled. "Maybe, sir, you want to get away from the noise." From several hundred yards away came the taped sounds of shouting voices, and horses' hooves clattering over cobblestones. "Awful to think we're to have ten straight nights of this."

"Awful," he agreed. He nodded, strolled past the guard and turned to his left. With a leap of his pulses he saw the slight figure perhaps a hundred yards ahead, a deeper dark against the darkness. He looked over his shoulder. No sign of the guard. Evidently he had moved farther back into the archway.

The little American snoop was just about to turn left toward the car park now. Landing on the balls of his feet at each long stride, he ran lithely forward. She had already turned the corner when he caught up with her. Apparently at the last moment she heard him, because she whirled around, mouth opening to scream.

He brought his fist against the point of her chin in an uppercut, and then caught her by the shoulders as she slumped. He bent, and hoisted the unconscious girl onto his shoulder in a fireman's lift. Carrying his burden, he plunged across a narrow deserted roadway toward Bushey Park. Near the spot where he came over the park wall that morning was a pile of brush. He would hide her body there, climb over the wall, and drive off in the Jaguar.

And after that? As long as he could keep that sniveling Kyle from taking control, he had nothing to worry about, because he was strong and clever, cleverer than all the rest of them, including the police, put together. And whenever he wanted to he could stay in control as long as was necessary. He'd done so the night he had given Cecily Grenville what was coming to her, hadn't he? He ran on, scarcely feeling the girl's weight.

Slowly, confusedly, she was regaining consciousness. For a few seconds she was aware only of the pain in her jaw and head. Then, eyes still closed, she realized with a leap of bewildered terror that she was being carried, not smoothly but with a jolting motion.

Her eyes flew open. She looked down at her own dangling arms and a dimly visible path below. Full awareness came to her then. A madman, jogging through the night, carried her over his shoulder, the same madman who had severed another girl's spinal cord with a blow of a cleaver.

At the last moment she was able to choke off the scream that had welled up in her throat. Her best course was to keep her mind clear, not give way to panic. There was a little light, perhaps from the stars, perhaps from a sliver of moon low in the west. She dared not turn her head to find out. But she could see tall grass at either side of the path, and randomly spaced trunks of trees. How long had she been unconscious? If only a few minutes, then surely they were still somewhere on the palace grounds, probably Bushey Park. But even in the daytime the farther reaches of Bushey Park were often so deserted that you could wander for half an hour without seeing anyone. After dark, the thousand acres of forest and thicket, empty of both visitors and guards, might as well be miles from nowhere.

What did he intend to do with her?

Don't think about it. Don't think of the knife descending, or the hands closing around her throat to choke off life. She must keep terror from clouding her mind. And she must keep pretending unconsciousness. The less on guard he was, this lunatic whose arms encircled her legs just above the knees, the more chance she would have of getting away from him.

Abruptly he halted. Heart thudding against the wall of her chest, she felt herself lowered until her feet touched the ground. His hands released her. Eyes still closed, she let her legs buckle at the knees, let herself fall backward. For a moment, as she lay motionless, there was silence. Then she heard his voice and felt the toe of his shoe nudge her, not urgently, in her left side.

"Open your eyes. I know you're awake."

What had betrayed her? Too rapid breathing? Or had he been able to hear, as she could, the hammering of her heart? Feeling the sweat roll down her sides she opened her eyes and smiled up at him through the dimness. "Please, Kyle."

That was a mistake. She knew it instantly, even though he answered her smile with a flash of his white teeth. "Kyle? Do I look like some prissy schoolmaster? Surely by now you can tell the difference between him and me. My name is M. Not E-m. Just M."

She forced her lips to hold that rigid smile. "I'm sorry. You do seem different from Kyle. But why do you want to hurt me? I never hurt you."

Instead of answering he extended his hands down to her. She grasped them—how strange that this murderer's hands felt as warm and firm as any other young man's—and allowed him to pull her to her feet.

He released her hands and then said softly, "You didn't do anything to me? You tried to get me shut away for life, that's all. And do you know what I'm going to do to you for that?"

Perhaps he would not have to kill her. Feeling the hammerlike beat of her heart, she knew that it was true that people could die from sheer terror. "Please," she whispered.

"What do you mean, please? What do you expect me to do? Let you go so you can help them have me locked up?"

No chance to dodge past him. He would merely reach out a long arm and scoop her in. No use to turn and try to run toward whatever lay behind her. He would overtake her with a couple of strides.

Swiftly she moved close to him and brought her knee up. Even more swiftly he moved backward and to one side. "Just full of tricks, aren't you?"

She saw the flat-handed blow coming and involuntarily let out a scream. His hand caught her across the cheek and knocked her to the ground. Ears ringing, but only vaguely aware of pain, she looked up at him. He stood motionless, as if waiting to see what she would do.

She scrambled to her hands and knees and then stood up. He still did not move, but just stood watching her. She whirled around. A brick wall only a few feet away. Bushey Park's wall? Whatever wall it was, there was a pile of brush beside it. If she could climb it, hoist herself to the top of the wall, drop to the other side—

She knew there was almost no chance she could do it. It would be a difficult feat even if he hadn't been there to haul her backward whenever he chose. But since she had no alternative, she ran forward. She hurled herself onto the pile of brush and, scrambling with both hands and feet, tried to crawl upward. Slipping and sliding, pulling one leg and then another free after they had broken into the pile, feeling twigs scratch her face, she clawed her way toward the top of the wall. Had something happened to him? Was that why he hadn't stopped her? She dared not take the time to look back at him, not when the top of the wall was almost within reach—

Sound of wood cracking underfoot. A hand at her collar, pulling her backward off the pile of brush. His other hand slapping her so hard that, when he released her collar, she staggered and fell to one knee.

He was grinning down at her. Weirdly, a memory from her seventh year flashed through her mind. The boy next door, and the ladybug he had imprisoned in a glass with about a quarter of an inch of water in the bottom. He would allow the water-soaked little creature to crawl almost to the rim of the glass, and then shake it down into the water again.

She got to her feet. Because he still had not moved, and because she had to keep trying to escape as long as she could, she darted away to the right. A grove of trees over there. If he allowed her to reach it, perhaps in the deeper darkness under the branches she could elude him for awhile.

She ran on for perhaps two seconds. Three. Four. Then, through the labored pounding of her heart, she heard the swish of his running footsteps through the long grass. His hand clutched her shoulder, spun her about.

She came around sobbing with despair, but fighting. Her fingernails reached out for his grinning face and furrowed down it, her knee aimed at his groin. He sidestepped, not grinning now, and with one blow knocked her to the ground. As she fell she realized, too late, that if she hadn't hurt him, hadn't clawed his face, he might have allowed her to live a little longer.

Then he was upon her, knees planted on either side of her body, long hands wrapped around her throat. Through the pain of those steely fingers squeezing her windpipe, through the roaring in her ears, she was aware that he was chanting words. "Annie and Cee-cee and Miss Judith Dunne, think they are three but to me are all one—"

The pain in her throat was nothing now. The true torment was in her lungs, laboring vainly to draw in life-sustaining air. Let it be quick, she prayed. Oh, please. Let it be quick.

For a few seconds after that crushing pressure on her throat ceased, her starved lungs were able to gulp in air, and she thought her silent petition had been granted. This surcease of torment came to you when you were dying.

Then, through the roaring that still persisted in her ears, she became aware of other sounds—feet scuffling over earth, impacts of fists against flesh, a man's voice shouting, "Over here!" and another man's cursing. Then there was silence except for the diminishing roar in her ears, and the pound of running footsteps, drawing closer.

She found that somehow she had managed to sit up. Figures seemed to swim through her blurred vision. A man lying on his back on the ground. Another man, tall, blond hair pale in the dimness—Steven? It couldn't be—standing over the man on the ground. Then two more men appeared out of the darkness and crouched beside the fallen man. After a moment she noted the visored caps they wore, and knew that they were guards.

The blond man said, "Can you get him onto his feet and start walking him back to the palace?" Dazed and incredulous, she realized that he really was Steven.

One of the guards answered, "We can give it a try, sir."

Steven was crouching beside her now. "Shall I carry you?"

She just looked at him, still not quite sure he was real. "Yes," he said, "I'd better. Put your arm around my neck."

"No!" Her mind had begun to function now.

"You mean you can walk?"

She nodded. She looked at the guards, moving away with the man who was not Kyle stumbling between them. Like most of the guards at Hampton Court, they were not young. Best that Steven be unburdened, so that he could help them if their prisoner began to struggle.

Steven drew her to her feet. Arm around her waist, he half-led, half-carried her along behind the men. She said, in a pain-thickened voice, "How on earth did you—"

"Don't try to talk. I'll tell you later."

As she and Steven moved past the deserted outdoor café, its white metal tables and chairs a ghostly glimmer in the darkness, she kept her apprehensive gaze fixed on the trio ahead. Dimly now she was aware of the sound of hooves galloping over earth, and of the ring of a lance against armor. The *son et lumière*, perhaps conjuring up the days when knights had ridden against each other in the area beyond the brick wall at her right, a tilting ground then but a flower garden now, breathing the fragrance of verbena and late roses into the dark. On the left was a tall yew hedge. The guards and their prisoner moved along it, and finally turned through an archway carved out of the shrubbery. She and Steven followed. She could see the three figures moving along the service area north of the palace wall.

Then, just before the guards and their prisoner reached the entrance to the passage that led to George Sherill's office, it happened. The slumped figure straightened, with one violent motion sent both guards staggering, and darted toward one of the tallest of the several aluminum ladders, one of which reached clear to the roof. Monkey-agile, he started to swarm up it.

Releasing her so abruptly that she almost fell, Steven ran forward. For a terrified moment she thought he was going to try to climb the same ladder. She pictured that madman pausing to kick his pursuer in the jaw, pictured Steven falling backward into space. Then, weak with relief, she saw that Steven had chosen another ladder, one only a few yards from where she stood.

The man who called himself M had stepped over the parapet onto the palace roof now. She expected him to flee out of sight of those on the ground, flee over the joined roofs of the vast structure in the hope of finding some means of descending the eastern wall of the palace, or the southern.

Instead he turned toward the top of the ladder the blond man was climbing.

"Steven!" The warning cry ripped out of her raw throat. But already the man on the roof had thrust the ladder outward from the wall. She saw Steven dropping through the air, knees flexed, upraised hands still gripping a rung of the ladder.

Then, as she stood paralyzed, she saw that the other man too was plummeting down through the night, falling from three times as great a height, arms still waving to regain the balance he had lost when he leaned over to thrust the ladder outward. Then the paralysis left her and she was able to lean against the wall and cover her face with her hands.

Seconds passed. Then she heard Steven's voice speak her name, felt him drawing her close to him. She took her hands down from her face and said numbly, "Then you're—"

"I'm fine. It wasn't much of a drop if you know how to land. And an aluminum ladder isn't heavy enough to hurt much even if you let it fall on you."

"And—and Kyle?"

"I don't know."

She turned away from Steven and moved toward where the two guards crouched beside the man lying on the ground. Steven made a protesting sound. Then, apparently changing his mind, he walked along beside her. She saw one of the guards rise and walk through the archway that led to George Sherill's office.

The remaining guard was shining a pocket torch now, not directly into the injured man's face but a little to one side. Nevertheless Judith could see clearly the trickle of blood coming from one corner of his mouth, and even the scratches her fingernails had made down one side of his face. And she could see his eyes—Kyle's eyes, brown and gentle and filled with unbearable anguish. He said, "Judith, were you badly hurt?"

Even without an injured throat she would have found it impossible to speak just then. She shook her head.

"It wasn't really I who did it, you know. For a long time now I've had a terrible feeling that there was someone else, but it's only now, when everything seems to be coming together in my mind, that I can remember the things he did."

"Please," she managed to say. "You shouldn't talk."

"It doesn't matter." His voice was calm. "I'm going to die anyway. I suppose that is why it has all come together in my mind. Perhaps the shock of knowing you're going to die is like the electric kind they give you in—"

His voice trailed off, and for a moment his eyes had an unfocused look. Then he said, "I did terrible things, or rather, that other one did." His gaze moved to Steven's face. "Your wife. I killed her."

200

Steven's voice too sounded as if it came from a tight throat. "Don't talk."

"It doesn't matter," he said again, but stopped speaking anyway, and after a moment Judith saw the brown eyes grow vacant and knew that he was dead.

No one spoke. George Sherill emerged from the archway that led to his office, exasperated alarm in his very walk. The other guard moved beside him.

Sherill halted and looked down at the figure on the ground. "What is all this? I step out of my office for a moment and then come back to find this man phoning for an ambulance and babbling something about an accident. Now tell me how this happened."

"The guards can tell you. I'm going to take Judith home."

Steven put his arm around her and led her toward the car park. Once more she became aware of amplified sounds. She heard a man's voice, feeble and peevish, and a woman's voice, brisk and motherly, and knew that only a hundred yards or so away an audience sat engrossed by Henry Tudor's last days with the last of his wives, the only one of the six who had been able to hold her own with him.

22

"JUDITH?"

She came groggily awake to find late morning sunlight streaming through the window. With momentary puzzlement she looked at Sister Naomi, the youngest of the Children of Emmanuel wives, standing in the bedroom doorway, freckled face smiling, carrot-colored braids dangling over thin shoulders. Then memory returned. Naomi had volunteered to spend the night on the sofa in Judith's living room.

"I fixed cereal and coffee for you," Naomi said. "They're on the stove. Is it all right if I go now? It's almost noon, and this is the day I give the little ones their weaving lesson."

"Of course." Talking was less painful this morning. "And thank you very much."

When Naomi had gone Judith still lay there, thinking of the night before. She and Steven, in his car, had left the palace grounds by a little-used gate in the Bushey Park wall and driven toward Hampton Court Village. From somewhere behind them came the wail of a siren. Judith knew it probably belonged to the ambulance the guard had summoned.

She had expected Steven to drive her home. Instead, despite her protests that all she needed was rest, he took her to Dr. Samuel Birdsley, the same man who had treated the cut on her leg. At sight of her swollen jaw and bruised throat, the little doctor's gaze swung to Steven. "First her leg and now this. What has been happening to this girl?"

Poor Steven, Judith thought, feeling a hysterical desire to laugh. For about a year now people had thought he might have been responsible for Cecily's death. And now, obviously, this doctor suspected he might be knocking *her* around.

Steven said, "What has been happening is over now."

No longer feeling an impulse toward laughter, Judith thought of the light going out of Kyle's eyes. Yes, it was over.

Steven went on, "I'll tell you about it while you're examining her."

He did tell a little about it, confining himself to that night's events—Kyle's assault upon her, and then his plunge from the palace roof. Dr. Birdsley, shining a light down Judith's throat, and gently touching her swollen jaw, made no comment except an occasional grunt until Steven had finished. Then he said, "I don't know whether the world is more violent than in the past. I'll leave that to the history and sociology Johnnies. But I do think there is a lot more irrational violence these days. Well, young lady, you've had a shock, but as far as your face and throat are concerned, you'll be as good as new in a few days."

Steven had driven her home then and, again over her protests, had rung the bell of the darkened main house until the light went on, and Brother John opened the door, with several of the other Children peering over his shoulder. Judith had suffered "an accident," he explained. Would one of the ladies stay in her apartment with her until morning? Naomi had volunteered, and Steven had driven off into the night.

Now she got out of bed and looked at herself in the dressing table mirror. Her face appeared a little less swollen but her throat looked even worse than it had the night before, with bruises ranging from dull red to purple. From the closet she took down a blue flannel dressing gown with a high ruffled neck and put it on. With her bruised throat hidden she looked almost normal.

She went into the kitchen, loaded a tray with the breakfast Naomi had prepared, and carried it back to the table beside the living room window. As she ate, finding even the soft cereal a little hard to swallow, she thought ahead to the next few days. Steven had said last night that he would ask the police to leave her alone until this afternoon, but she would have to see them. Sometime very soon she would have to go to poor Mrs. Hodge. And of course she would have to testify at the inquest. But after that?

Well, she thought gloomily, she might as well go to New York. True, if it had not been for Steven Grenville, she would be dead now. After they left the palace he had been solicitous for her welfare in a cool, stern sort of way. But that was all. There had been nothing in his manner to indicate that he wanted her to stay in England.

She went to the phone, called Pan Am, and changed her seat on that afternoon's flight for one a week away. Probably, she thought, as she hung up, the airline again would allow her to take her drawing case into the cabin with her—

Her drawing case! Where was it? She'd had it with her when she walked out of the palace the night before. She must have dropped it when she was attacked. But where was it now? All those drawings, weeks and weeks of work—

She told herself not to be too alarmed. There was little chance that anyone beside guards and administrative personnel had been in that part of the palace grounds last night. No doubt one of them had kept the case for her, or perhaps turned it over to George Sherill. The thing to do was to call George's office.

She had lifted the phone and started to dial when she heard footsteps on the outdoor staircase. Knuckles rapped softly and Steven's voice called, "Judith?"

Heartbeats rapid, she went to the door and opened it. He stood there, not smiling, with her drawing case in his hand. "I thought you might be asleep."

"No, I've finished breakfast. Come in, please." As he followed her into the living room she added, "I was just about to phone the palace about my case, but I see you have it."

"One of the guards had taken charge of it. The lock hadn't burst open, so I imagine you'll find all your work intact."

He stood the case on the table near the window and then, at Judith's invitation, sat down beside her on the sofa. He said, "They've located Mrs. Hodge's sister."

"Sara Smeaton?"

"Yes. I heard about it at the police station this morning. She's in a hospital in Gorman, partially paralyzed by a stroke and unable to speak. It happened in a compartment of a London-bound train."

Just what, Judith wondered, had occurred in that train compartment? Well, unless Sara Smeaton regained the ability to communicate, no one might ever know.

She said, "When do the police want to see me?"

"About half an hour from now, at two o'clock. I can drive you to the palace, so that you can pick up your car before you see the police."

"Thank you." She paused and then said, "You still haven't told me how you happened to be in Bushey Park last night."

"It wasn't a case of happenstance. I'd come to the palace looking for you."

He told her how, over steak-and-kidney pie in a pub, he had played back their conversation of several hours earlier. "It seemed to me that you might have gained some rather—risky knowledge about Cecily's death. After I called this number and got no answer, I thought of driving out here. Then, since it was nearer, I decided to go to the palace first. Thank God I did. I went to Sherill's office and he told me you'd said you intended to work in the State Apartments."

Crossing Fountain Court, Steven had met a guard who told him that he had seen her leaving the apartments about a quarter of an hour before. Sure that she must have gone out onto the grounds through the eastern entrance, Steven went there. Yes, the guard on duty told him, she had left only minutes ago.

"I was sure you'd gone to the car park, so I started after you. Then, when I turned the corner of the palace, I saw your drawing case on the ground. I knew you would never have dropped it unless you had been under some sort of attack." He stopped speaking for a moment, his stomach knotted with the memory of the fear he had felt.

"I also knew," he went on, "that your attacker would not have taken you to the car park, not when he'd have been sure to encounter at least a few people there. I ran across the road toward Bushey Park. A couple of guards saw me. They'd just finished their shift, I guess, and were going toward the car park. Anyway, when I told them what the trouble was, they of course volunteered to help."

Fanning out, with about fifty yards between them, the

three men had gone deep into Bushey Park. "From some-place far off I heard you scream. I was the first one to reach you, but by the time I'd hauled him off you and managed to knock him down, the two guards were there too."

She said, into the silence, "If there was only some way to thank—"

"No need for that," he said curtly. He got to his feet and stood looking down at her. "Do you still plan to go to New York?

"Yes. I've just made a plane reservation for next week."

"Why? Have you decided that you really do love that writer fellow? I know I have no right to ask that, but I'm asking anyway."

You could have every right, she thought bitterly, if you wanted to claim it. Even if you would just look at me gently, instead of in that aloof way—Aloud she said, "I'd rather not answer that."

As if some long-maintained defenses had crumbled, that aloof look in his eyes gave way to a strangely compli-cated expression, ashamed and pleading and yet stub-born. "Don't go."

After a moment she managed to say, "Why not?"

"Maybe I can't give you a reason that's good enough. I can't say, 'Stay here and marry me.' After what my first marriage was, I may not want to marry anyone else for a long time, not even you. And yet I think we could come to love each other. At least I know I already love you. And so unless you feel you can't live without this Barney what's-his-name, stay here and take a chance with me."

She looked at him, unable to speak. In the silence the phone rang. She lifted it, and heard a man's voice say that he had an overseas call for her. And then, as if Steven's words had become some sort of telepathic communica-

207

tion across the Atlantic, Barney's voice asked, "Judith, are you all right?"

She said, bewildered, "Yes. But how—"

"I just woke up and while the coffee was perking I tuned in the seven o'clock news. There was this story about some psycho at Hampton Court Palace who'd attacked an American artist and then died in a fall from the roof. The story gave your name. Judith, are you sure you're all right?"

"Of course I'm sure. A bit bruised, but all right."

"And your illustrations? Did anything happen to them? I mean, if you had your drawing case with you when it happened—"

Lips curved in a wry smile, she looked at the case standing on the table. "Yes, they're okay. I finished the last one yesterday."

"You've finished them? Hey! That's fantastic. Why don't you ship them off to me right away? I mean, you won't want to come back just yet, not when you planned to stay until September."

After a long moment she said, "You can scarcely wait to see me, can you?" When he did not speak she added, "Okay, Barney. Come clean."

He gave a groan. "I should have known I couldn't fool you. Well— These things happen, Judith, they happen. I met this girl—her father is senior editor at Hudson House Books, and, well—"

His voice trailed off. She said gently, "I understand. I'll send you the drawings. As for the rest of it—"

"Yes?"

"As for the rest of it, Barney, go fly your kite."

She hung up.

After a moment Steven asked, in a strained voice, "Did that mean what I hope it meant?"

"It did."

"Then you'll take a chance on us? You'll stay?"

Stay! She'd decided to stay even before the phone rang a few minutes ago.

She saw the hope in the gray eyes that used to seem to her so cold and remote. She remembered that rainy morning when, fingers biting into her shoulders, he had looked down at her with a blend of anger and desire. And she knew that, no matter what he himself believed at the moment, she really wouldn't be taking a chance at all.

"Yes," she said. "I'll stay."